FREEDOM

K. Lissa Cordova

authorHOUSE®

AuthorHouse™
1663 Liberty Drive
Bloomington, IN 47403
www.authorhouse.com
Phone: 1 (800) 839-8640

Published by AuthorHouse 08/11/2020

ISBN: 978-1-7283-6556-5 (sc)
ISBN: 978-1-7283-6571-8 (e)

Print information available on the last page.

This book is printed on acid-free paper.

CONTENTS

PRAISE FOR FREEDOM

Lissa is an exceptional and genuine writer. Her words bring color and history experiences to life. As we journey through this book, with the eyes and heart of Emma (Lissa), we are going not only to enjoy this book, but also receive helpful guidance to everyday life experiences. And most importantly; this book brings hope, healing, and teaches us that it's never too late to start your life over.

Laura Diaz
Author of La Novia en Servicio
Pastor, Fruit of The Vine Church Tampa, FL

"Now our hope for you is unshakable, because we know that just as you share in sufferings you will also share in God's comforting strength." (Corinthians 1:7, PTP). The hope that we have in Christ is unshakable! It is unshakable even in the darkest moments where freedom was not part of the room we were dwelling in! In the midst of those moments…full of sufferings it is where Lissa met the One who had the key to open the door to freedom. That door is not only available to Lissa but to you as well. I pray that as you read this book, "Freedom", you will finish the last chapter knowing that God has been and always will be there for you.

Zoah Calveti
Founder of Mustard Books

"Freedom" is a story of hope in midst of fear and desolation. This book is medicine to the wounded heart that seeks liberty from abuse. God can use our wounds for a greater purpose. I highly recommend this book not only for women but everyone who needs an answer when the road in life seems difficult to see.

Michael Cordova
Author of Sole Se Vive Una Vez
Ma, Counseling in Psychology
Pastor of Vida en Familia

"Freedom" is a powerful exploration of one woman's return to empowerment through faith. Cordova's journey reflects a powerful universal message to anyone who has been disempowered, or lost their way, that it is possible to find solace and strength in the divine, and in themselves.

Amy Jayalakshmi Hellman
Co Author of Amazon #1 Best-sellers "Heal Thy Self," and "Empower Your Life."
Theta Healing Certificate of Science and Master Instructor, Teacher and Certified Sivananda and Vinyasa Yoga Instructor. Certified Thai Yoga Bodyworker

Lissa writes from the heart. In her words, she captures emotions so many have felt but have struggled to give voice to. I believe this piece will set people free, lead to restoration in relationships, and begin a journey of growing closer to God that many have longed for or are just discovering.

Nicholas Mustakas
Pastor

Lissa does an amazing job in depicting the inner struggle we all experience in reconnecting with our true self and God. I find Emma and her challenges to be extremely relatable. We all lose ourselves for one reason or another, and while our journey to find ourselves once again may all differ, the only True Way to "Freedom" remains the same for everyone!

Beth Webb
Student and servant of Jesus Christ
B.S. Psychology & Christian Counseling

DEDICATION

This book is written to honor God, our Holy Father who trusted me to deliver His message.

To my daughter Ashley, who taught me to look at myself from the outside in, and to fight for my life.

To all the women in the world; may you be as happy as God intended.

INTRODUCTION

Writing my first book was not easy. It was more emotional than I thought it would be. I took long breaks in between each chapter so that I could focus on each topic and write it well. I needed to breathe. It didn't help that I didn't believe in myself. When you read this book, you will understand why. Why? I didn't think anyone would want to hear what I had to say, or how I could possibly make a difference in someone's life, be a positive influence, or an inspiration. Doubt is a terrible thing. Confidence is a great thing that comes from having faith. I was able to finish only when I listened to God's voice telling me to use the gift He gave me to write and inspire women.

This book is about a girl and her will to survive the difficult life she was given, the choices she'd made throughout, and her journey to understand it all. What she didn't expect was to find solace in God's love throughout her journey.

ACKNOWLEDGMENTS

To God; thank You for restoring my faith, and for the lessons that prepared me to understand and follow my purpose. Thank you for your love and patience.

To my beautiful daughter, Ashley; God blessed me with you and I thank Him every day. Thank you for your loving spirit. You inspire me with your strength, your drive, and awareness of life.

To my brother, Pastor Michael Cordova; your big sister looks up to her younger brother. You have taught me how to listen to God, and the power of His love.

To my sister in law, Pastor Everidis Morales Cordova; thank you for making me aware that I had the tools all along to be free when you told me to 'fly.' "You have wings, Fly!" you said.

To my parents, my siblings, and my nieces and nephews; you have all taught me something, and have inspired me in so many ways. I love you all!

To my big sister, Kim Manfra; you believed in me more than I believed in myself. Thank you for never giving up on us.

To my sister, Heidi R. Cordova; God put you in my life at the right time. Thank you for always being there.

To the women, my sisters in Christ from The Journey Church. You taught me what the true meaning of friendship is. Thank you for believing in my vision for "The Journey Foundation, Inc."

"Where the Spirit of the Lord is, there is Freedom." 2 Corinthians 3:1

CLARITY

It was a cool Monday morning in October, when Emma waved goodbye to her fiancé, Mitch as he left for a business trip. With a sigh of relief, she closed the door behind her pushing out the cold air. She closed her eyes for a moment, and laid against the door hoping he wouldn't come back. She waited for about a minute and felt the nervousness disappear once she was sure he wouldn't come back. Emma peeled her body away from the door, and walked in darkness towards the kitchen. She was exhausted physically and emotionally from the minute events of everyday life.

While in the kitchen she made herself a cup of tea as she moved in what seemed to be slow motion. She sat down with her tea and took in the silence of the room. It comforted her. She felt empty and hopeless as if she had left her body, and allowed it to feel whatever it wanted. Her chair was facing the doors that lead to the yard so she slowly focused her sight on the early morning darkness.

She whispered, "Oh Emma, what has become of your life?" She didn't recognize herself anymore. Words her father once told her when she was a teen popped into her head. "Emma, God is always with us. If you need something just ask Him." She never asked God for anything except for 'why' on occasion when something bad happened, but she never understood that she could actually ask God to help her. She decided to put it to the test. Putting her cup of tea down, she walked slowly to the door, opened it, and stepped outside to feel cold air on her face. Arms hanging at her sides in defeat, she took this time to ask God for something, but she just didn't know what it was that she needed. "God, it's me, Emma." She realized at that very moment she didn't need to know what she needed from God because He did. Not another word came out of her mouth before she cried uncontrollably. He was there...she felt Him. He had been waiting for her the whole time...she felt it in her soul. Her body shivered as she fell to her knees in surrender. She did not understand it fully, but she knew it was God. It was an undeniable presence. She felt the light of the rising sun shine through her, and a strength she had never felt in her life. "Emma," she said out loud, "it's time."

She was done with this life. She wanted a new one. When she was calm, she got up, and wiping her tears went inside the house. The sunlight shone throughout the kitchen. She swore it was brighter than she had ever seen it, but that could be because she had never really noticed it before. She grabbed her laptop, straightened her shoulders, and turned it on. With all the confidence in the world, she simply let God guide her. Without even thinking about why, she opened a browser, and let the Holy Spirit move her. The cursor was blinking in the Google search bar, and she typed each letter slowly; "U-n-i-t-e-d A-i-r-l-i-n-e-s." That was the beginning of the realization that it was time to go home. The tears pouring out of her were of happiness, relief, anger, confusion, disappointment, frustration, and embarrassment. "You can do this, Emma... you deserve to be happy." She never believed that before... never thought it possible. For her whole life she had been used and pushed around. She tried to remember the last time she was truly happy. Not many thoughts came to her other than memories of her sisters in New York, her brother David (who she was raised with), her baby sister Raquel (the little girl she left behind), and the birth of her daughter Lyla. FAMILY - that's what it came down to. Life had been stolen from her. That's how the devil works, and she let it happen - that included Mitch. He had done the most damage to her, and it was time to take her life back! She was in her 40's, but she didn't care - it was better now than never. She had not lived her own life. Other people, like Mitch, manipulated hers.

"They had to know they were hurting me God, didn't they? Or were they really so selfish and self-involved?" She pictured herself covered in pieces of a black puzzle, and for the first time those puzzle pieces were falling off her body from head to toe to reveal glowing colors. This will take some time she thought, but HOPE, had returned to her life. She would stop this life dead in its tracks, and start anew. She didn't know how that would happen yet, but she was beginning to have faith again. Looking at the screen on her laptop, she suddenly felt light headed.

"What am I doing?" she asked herself. She took a deep breath and typed in some dates, and a city to search for airline tickets. Once she found what felt right, she paused and held her finger over the "purchase" button. She had some money saved, and this was the time to use it. She closed her eyes for a second, then opened them, and quickly clicked that button. She pulled her hand back as if the keyboard were on fire, and put her hands over her mouth in surprise of what she had just done.

"Oh my Gosh, I just bought a plane ticket!" She felt a surge of positive energy flow through her body, and she screamed. She had never done anything like this before. She couldn't even remember when she had last made a decision for herself. She thanked God for the courage she suddenly was given. Standing up, she looked at the bedroom mirror, smiled, and said, "You did it! I don't know what you did, but you did it!" Just as quickly as she felt happy, a wave of fear came over her...another tactic of the enemy was to make people doubt themselves. She felt dizzy and overwhelmed as doubt and fear slowly started to fill her mind. "No!" she said. She would not stop now... she couldn't - especially realizing what Mitch was doing to her, and what he was capable of.

"Okay, Emma, think. What do we do now? Mitch will come home, and won't let you leave. There is no way he will allow it." Realizing how much control she allowed Mitch to have over her life angered her. She would have to figure that out later, but now she needed a plan of escape. She closed her eyes, and prayed again. That seemed to help. "God do you agree that I need to do this? I don't know what else to do or how, nor do I know right from wrong anymore." She grabbed her phone, and called her father.

"Hello." She heard her father answer the phone, and felt a pain in her heart. She missed him so much. "Hi Dad, it's Emma." She asked for his blessing like she was accustomed to doing. "Bendicion." Her voice was shaky.

"God bless you, Honey. How are you? It's been a long time...so glad to hear from you." Al knew his daughter well, and thought that something was up as he heard it in her voice. "Baby, is everything okay?" "No Dad." She started to cry. Al never heard her like this before. "Emma, what's wrong baby?" Then he heard the words he was longing for.

"I need to come home, Dad." Tears welled up in her dad's eyes, and there was a long pause. "Dad…?" She waited, and figured he was in shock since she had not called in a while... shame on her. His voice was shaky.

"Are you kidding? Of course, come home. I miss you so much! I am here for you, and will always be. Just tell me when, and I'll be there to pick you up." Al had not always been there, but he had a big heart, and was very loving. She knew the difference between then and now, and now - he was there for her. She heard excitement but also sadness in her dad's voice, and it surprised her even though it shouldn't have. He loved her. Emma had forgotten that fact because she was so emotionally involved with Mitch, and separated herself and her feelings from others. The realization that she had not only neglected herself but her family as well angered her even more.

"Umm, is tomorrow too soon?" She heard her dad laugh in response. "What?! Oh my gosh! It is never too soon. Wow. I can't believe it! This is so awesome, Honey!" "Thanks, Dad. I stayed away too long. I'm sorry." "Honey, I sensed something was wrong when I didn't hear from you very often. For right now just text the details to me, and I will be at the airport waiting for you, probably with everyone." She laughed at that. She missed her culture. That's how it was in Puerto Rico...family oriented and loving. All she heard from Mitch was how they didn't need family...they had each other. He was wrong! When she hung up the phone, she felt a bit more relieved and empowered. She called her daughter to tell her what was going on. Lyla supported her all the way.

"It's about time, Mom! I just wish you had done it when I was little - we both went through that rollercoaster of emotions." Guilt… Emma would have to deal with that later too. She knew she wasn't alone, even though Mitch wanted her to believe that. Right now she needed to get away without him knowing, or he would talk her out of it. She was not sure that she was ready to take on the journey of her life, but she put God in control and started to pack. She left the bag in the hall closet just in case he flew back unexpectedly.

As she closed the closet door, the sound of the phone startled her and made her jump. She hated how nervous he made her. She stared at her cell phone, took a deep breath, and picked it up. "Hello? Honey, it's me!" She cringed. His voice was no longer pleasing to her. "I'm going to stay a few more days. We have some problems I need to handle, okay? I already changed my ticket so I'll see you in a few days." He hung up as if in a hurry without her even acknowledging. She stared at her phone in disbelief.

"Did he just say he was staying a few more days?!?" she asked out loud. She felt her body relax, and could not believe the blessing she had just received. "Thank you, God!." She started to care less and less about how Mitch might react, but there was still that feeling of responsibility... that she owed him something. She wrote a quick note explaining how she felt and why she left that she would send to him when she was on her way to the airport. In the meantime, she grabbed her laptop, went downstairs to the dining room, made a tuna sandwich, and sat down. She opened her laptop to a blank page in "Microsoft Word" and stared at the screen. Emma was a writer at heart. It was something she was good at, but never had the opportunity to explore the way she had wanted. If what she wanted to do had nothing to do with Mitch, then she didn't do it. "Ugh!" she said to herself. Today was a new day. Anything seemed possible, so she began to type. She started with making two lists:

1. Life goals
2. My accomplishments

When she was finished, she sat back to compare the two. She was faced with the reality of not having lived. "What did that mean?" she thought. She needed to think, and to sort everything out. The more she realized it, the angrier she became with herself and the whole situation. She needed this trip. Booking the trip alone was a big step in the right direction. Emma was filled with determination. She cleaned up, and left a note for Mitch which was more like a letter explaining that she needed a break. She got her coat, grabbed her bag, and headed to the airport that same morning.

She couldn't stay in his house another minute. She decided to stay at a hotel near the airport so it would be easier for her the next morning, and she wouldn't have to face Mitch, and have her day ruined. At the hotel she started to think about how she had arrived at this moment. She thought about her life, how she grew up, and of the experiences that perhaps made her submissive and accepting of the misery in her life. "How did this happen?" she asked out loud. It was important that she understand how so many years had gone by without her living them.

"Okay, Emma...think!" She knew it was time to go back in time to figure out how she managed to arrive here. How did she become this person who gave up so much power to others? It was time to get focused and to get her life back.

TWO PEAS IN A POD

It was the 70's. Fall had arrived, there were leaves on the ground, and a light breeze filled the air. A new school year had begun. There would be a sea of kids heading to school with their pencil cases filled with freshly sharpened pencils and clean erasers, their backpacks stuffed with notebooks of blank pages ready to be filled with information, and the butterflies that kids felt on their first day of school.

One afternoon, the curly haired little girl with yellow ribbons could not wait any longer. She anxiously rocked back and forth on her heels. "Mommy where is it?" she asked. "It's not coming, Mommy!" Susan was holding her son, David while Emma whined. "It will be here any moment, Honey...don't worry." "Whennnn?" Emma wailed. Then she saw it! The big yellow school bus was coming down the street. She squealed with excitement! Emma wasn't old enough to ride the bus yet, but she couldn't wait to be on it someday, and sit right next to her big sister, Katie. She jumped up and down waiting for the bus to stop so that she could see her sister. Her mother smiled. She enjoyed how excited Emma got when her sister came home. She knew that she looked up to Katie, and hoped it would always stay that way. Finally, the bus stopped. Emma ran up to the door waiting for Katie to come out. "Katieeeee!" Emma yelled. Katie smiled when she got off the bus, and held out her arms. It was routine that she would gleefully run into them. Katie enjoyed every minute of the attention. She adored her little sister. Wherever she went Emma went, and she never minded. "I was waiting for you Katie." She grabbed her sister. Even though Katie was only two years older than Emma, she felt the need to take care of her. "Thank you for waiting for me." Susan gave Katie a kiss hello. "Come on girls, let's get home, and make dinner. You guys can help set the table. Katie, make sure to hold Emma's hand when we cross the street, okay?" "Okay, Mom, I will," she replied. The girls walked up the hill singing the *Jackson 5*'s version of "Rockin' Robin".

Emma was shy, but a bit wild. She was hyperactive, smart, curious, and very observant. Katie was more outgoing, and even more hyperactive than Emma. You put the two of them together and it spelled "T-R-O-U-B-L-E." They were fearless. Their neighborhood was their playground. They had a lot of freedom as children, and one of them would always come home with some sort of scrape. It still did not stop them from having fun.

"Emma, stop bothering David," their mother said. "Mom, he's a whiny baby." David was crying, and annoyed with Emma because she was teasing him, and taking his toy cars. "But Mom, I want to play with his cars." "He's playing with them, Emma...leave him be." She continued bothering him until little David had enough. With a little baby tantrum, he picked up one of his toy cars and threw it at Emma. She screamed and covered her face. Her mom and dad ran to her. "Emma, let me see...move your hand," Al said, trying to see the damage. "Is she ok, Al?" Susan asked.

"I'm going to have to take her to the emergency room." Her left eye was covered in blood. Al picked up Emma, and ran with her to the hospital as quickly as possible, while Susan stayed with the other kids. Al anxiously waited to hear from the doctor. When he finally came out to greet him, he jumped up. "How is she?" he asked. "She was frightened as you might imagine. It's not your normal injury, but we got her to calm down, and were able to assess the damage." He continued, "There is some scarring in the eye, and she's bruised in the surrounding area, but overall, she should be fine. We just need to keep her here for observation." Al nodded in agreement. "Can I see her?"

The doctor walked him into Emma's room. She looked so frail with both eyes bandaged. She had obviously been crying, and was sucking her thumb as if to soothe herself. The doctor whispered to Al, "It looks worse than it is." Al got closer to Emma's bed. "Hi, Honey." Emma took her thumb out of her mouth, and sat up quickly. She tried to pull up the bandage from her good eye to see her father, and began to cry. Her dad held her gently. "It's ok, Honey. Your eye is a little hurt so you need to keep the bandages on, okay?" She continued to cry, and hold on to her dad. "No, Daddy. I wanna go home." The doctor spoke, "Emma if you leave those bandages on for a few days, you can go home sooner." She shook her head no, but she knew she had to stay. During her stay, her parents visited often, and her mom brought her a little basket of flowers with butterflies and a little bumble bee sticking out of it. She loved it and kept it with her at all times. If she couldn't be with her parents, she would hold on to the bumble bee while they were apart.

The hospital stay did not stop Emma. As soon as she got home, she was her own hyper self. "Emma, get down from there you can't reach," called out Emma's mother. "I got her, Mom," Katie yelled back as if her 8-year-old self was so much older. But before you knew it, Emma came tumbling down from the monkey bars. She hit her chin on one of the bars before she hit the floor. "Oh no! I told you! Katie, go get your father. I have to stay with the babies." Katie ran to get her dad who took Emma to the hospital once again. When she finally got back home after being patched up, her mother looked at her bandaged chin, and gave her a kiss. "I got 6 stitches, Mommy!" Emma said proudly. "I told you those monkey bars are too high for you...try the lower one's next time." But she was not having it. "No, Mom, that one is for babies. I like the high ones. Wait until you see me hang upside down!" Katie put her index finger to her lips as if to shoosh her, and Emma caught on. "Oh, never mind I don't know how to do that." Her mom made a face at Katie. "Oh, I know what you two are up to." They ran to their room, and Susan laughed. A few days later they were at it again.

"Let's go, Emma," Katie yelled out. "I'm coming...I'm coming," Emma answered from inside the hallway. She had pony tails and one of them was falling out...yellow ribbons stringing behind her. Katie grabbed the Big Wheel, and waited for Emma to hop on in the back. "You ready, Emma? You're gonna love this!" Emma trusted Katie, and would do anything she said. She ran out to meet her, then stopped. "Wait, I need my shoes." She started to run back into the apartment building. "Just come on...we don't need shoes! Hurry before Daddy comes over!" Emma didn't know what that meant. Why couldn't Daddy see them? She ran over to her sister, and hopped on the back of the Big Wheel. "Okay, let's go fast!" Katie said as Emma grabbed on to her sister's waist. They took off down the hill, and heard a voice in the background. "Hey, where are you guys going?" Al could already see the imminent danger in their little ride. He ran after them, but was too late. The girls were on their way down the steep hill by their apartment in the Jersey Street housing projects at the highest speed a Big Wheel could possibly go...barefoot!

"Stop!" he yelled out as he ran. He wondered how a Big Wheel could go so fast! "Uh oh!" said Katie as she realized that they were heading toward the main road of Richmond Terrace onto incoming traffic. "What's, uh oh?" Emma asked but Katie looked preoccupied. "Just hold on, Emma!" Emma heard the nervousness in her sister's voice. "No, you said uh oh! What's happening?!"

"Quick, we need to stop...cars are coming!" Emma felt a knot in her stomach. "Stop?! It's a Big Wheel, it doesn't have brakes." All the girls could do now was try to stop on their own and they instantaneously put their feet down on the concrete to stop the speeding Big Wheel. It still was not stopping fast enough so Katie had to do something else. "Plan B!" She yelled out. Emma didn't flinch and followed her sisters lead and held on tight. Katie turned the wheel a hard-right towards the grass, but then she remembered that the grass was guarded by chains which were at their head level and her eyes widened. She yelled out to Emma. "Emma, duck!" Both girls put their heads back, and drove right under the chains onto the grass. They were crying, nervous, and in excruciating pain. Their feet were skinned raw from the street.

"Are you crazy?" Al cried out as he ran over to see the damage. He put his hands on his hips while catching his breath, relieved that their heads were still attached to their bodies. He heard Susan yell out through the apartment window.

"Al, their feet! Check their feet! I told them to put their shoes on this morning." It was the first time Katie and Emma were actually afraid, since not much else scared them. They were both crying. "Daddy, it hurts." Al picked them up, and took them inside. Their feet were badly injured, and

Emma's left thigh was burned from the back tire of the Big Wheel. They couldn't walk for weeks. Although they learned their lesson that day, it still didn't stop them from being daring.

Emma and Katie continued their shenanigans, and it was about a year later that Emma had to take another trip to the hospital.

"Mom, can I ride with Johnny?" Emma asked her Mother...she knew it was a stretch. Johnny was a kid from the neighborhood. He was the only one with a bike, and Emma wanted to ride on it. "Only if you ride around where I can see you." Emma jumped on the back of Johnny's bike...it was a 10 speed! She wouldn't stop bugging him until he agreed to ride her around the park. "Yay, Johnny let's go!" Johnny was delighted. "Ok Emma you ready? Hold on tight." She held onto Johnny as they rode around the park. Suddenly she felt a sharp pain, and squeezed Johnny as a reflex. "What's wrong, Emma?" She didn't cry but was breathing hard, and her eyes were wide open as if she was trying to hold the pain in. She didn't know what to do. Words were not coming out of her mouth. "Stop! Her foot is stuck," someone had shouted. Johnny very nervously stopped the bike, but it fell over to the left where Emma's foot was stuck.

"Mom, it hurts!" Her mom came over to help. People surrounded them trying to extract her foot from the spokes. "Sit still, Emma, we're getting your foot out." She was trying to be brave at 7 years old, but the pain was too much. The tears flowed. It was time for another Emergency Room visit.

The doctor declared, "It's not broken, but it is definitely sprained. Wear this wrap around it and stay off your foot." Emma crossed her fingers behind her back, and Katie giggled.

THE WITCH'S HOUSE

They were at a new house now, on Hamilton Avenue in St. George, Staten Island. The girls loved it. They had a yard where they would have barbecues with friends, and Emma loved stomping on cranberries that fell to the ground from the tree. It was like red paint on the ground.

"Emma, stop that! It stains the ground...don't do that." Emma turned around to see her beautiful mother with her long dark hair. She was mesmerized by her mother's beauty. "Okay, sorry, Mom," she said as she stomped on the last cranberry, and ran over to her dad. "Dad, can we go today?" Al grinned and said, "You know, Honey, if we sit here near the window, we can watch the game." Emma loved listening to the sounds of the marching band, and the football team from Curtis High School across the street. She would watch the kids run track with her dad sometimes too. She wanted to join them. She loved to run, and she was good at it.

Since it was summer and schools were closed, the girls spent a lot of time outdoors exploring the neighborhood. One of their favorite things to do was to sneak into the high school, and put on band hats. They would fit their skinny little bodies in between the top of the fence and ceiling to gain access to the band room. If they weren't doing such 'death defying' things elsewhere, they would have fun at home. "Daddy, we love it!" the girls said. Al had turned the old attic into a bedroom for them, and even used their mother's United Kingdom flag as a curtain for the window. The room was perfect!

Winters were difficult for the girls because they couldn't be outside for too long. "Emma, where are you?" Katie called out. She heard Emma in the distance. "In here!" In the corner of their room in the attic was a small door that led to a closet that appeared to have been used as a tiny office. There were papers, books, and files everywhere. Emma was intrigued. "Katie, look at all this stuff." Katie looked around. "All I see are dusty old papers and books. They must have belonged to the people that used to live here. Come on, Emma, let's watch TV." 'The Brady Bunch' is on." Emma stayed a minute before she ran after her sister.

"Who wants vanilla pudding with whipped cream?" Susan yelled out. Almost in unison the girls yelled back, 'Me!" "Okay, let me just put the little ones to bed first." The girls turned back to the TV. "Katie, I'm cold. Are you cold too?" she asked as she folded her arms to her chest. "Yes, I'm cold too." Their mom popped up with their delicious dessert. "Okay, eat your pudding. Then after this show, brush your teeth and head to bed okay?" They took the pudding and nodded. "Mom, it's cold in here...can you turn the heat on?" Susan knew it was cold, but she pretended that she wasn't aware. The heat was cut off since they were unable to pay the last few bills. Al wasn't home, and it wasn't the first time he was out late. "Okay, I will check it out. Remember, bed time after this." It was after midnight when Susan bundled all the kids in her bed. It was very cold in the house, and the kids kept waking up. She feared that if Al didn't do something about this, they would have no food left either. Even with food stamps it was tough to get by with four children and a missing husband.

Katie was mature, more so than anyone gave her credit for and noticed everything. She made sure to protect her siblings, and prayed that her parents would care enough to protect her. One afternoon she and Emma were playing when they heard a very loud knocking on the door. Emma ran and hid in a corner because she knew it was the old lady who owned the house. She was banging her cane on the glass window of the door, and calling out Susan's name. She was loud and mean. She reminded Emma of the Wicked Witch of the West from "The Wizard of Oz." "I already paid you, Mrs. McGuire. Go away, you're scaring my kids!" As Susan walked away from the door, she found Emma curled up hiding under a table. She helped her up. "Mom, I don't like that lady," Emma said, shaking. "It's okay, Emma. She can't come in, and I will call her son to let him know. She has dementia." Emma didn't know what that was, but she knew her mom would protect her.

The old house held both good and bad memories for Emma. Summers were hot, but Emma loved it because she could be outside all day long. She felt free! The summer also reminded her of Puerto Rico where her father's side of the family lived. They visited several times, and for Emma, it was a happy place to be. "Katie, let's go to the park. I wanna get lunch." Being welfare kids had its benefits, free lunch during the summer and free lunch at school. "Maybe we can find Dad...he's probably playing basketball."

Their dad wasn't home very much, but they knew they could find him with his karate buddies or at the basketball court. "Hey, Daddy," Emma yelled out. Al looked up from playing, and waved at her. "Are you gonna come home later, Dad?" He gave her a nod as he threw the ball to his buddy. "Don't leave without me, okay?" she continued, then ran to play when he agreed. She kept an eye on him because he tended to disappear a lot. When she saw him packing up and putting on his t-shirt, she ran to him. "You ready, Dad?" He looked at her, signaled to his friends, and told Emma to go home. "No, Daddy, I want to go with you." Al knew Emma was stubborn, and it would be difficult to get rid of her. Katie was more understanding, or rather she had given up hope on him being a normal dad. "Katie, grab your sister." She shook her head no. She was tired of his games.

Emma wasn't the only one who missed him. He managed to sneak away when Emma turned her head. She cried as she chased his car down the street. The girls walked home and as soon as Emma got there, she went to her mother. "Mom, Daddy drove away. I told him to wait for me, Mom. It's not fair!" "None of this is fair." Susan whispered to herself. "It's okay, Honey. Go watch TV. I'm making pudding." That's all Emma needed to hear. She wiped her tears, and went to watch TV.

A few months later Susan got the news that her husband was not coming home. He had left her to live with his parents in Puerto Rico. "Mom, where's Dad?" Emma asked her mom who was rummaging through cabinets looking for food for her children. Al had left her with nothing, and God only knows what he had told his family about her. They probably blamed her, Susan thought. "Honey, not right now...go play with the kids." Emma folded her arms across her chest in an upset manner and stomped her foot. "Mom, but I want Daddy!" Susan knew the kids didn't truly understand what was happening, but it bothered her that they wanted their father. After all, he had abandoned his family when they needed him the most. Emma grabbed some sugar from the sugar bowl to eat. "Katie, I'm hungry but all I could find was sugar," she said, licking her little fingers. Katie was starving too. "It's okay, Emma. Mom will figure something out. When we go to school, we will have breakfast and lunch, okay?" Emma nodded rather easily distracted, and ran over to her little brother to play with him.

LITTLE BROKEN SOULS

"Mom, why did Santa give me a Marie Osmond doll? I wanted Donny! Was it because I was bad when I stole gum from the..?" Katie squeezed Emma's hand hard to stop her from talking. Susan looked at Emma in surprise. "What? You stole what?!" Emma turned pale. "Umm, nothing. I mean I had a dream I stole gum, Mom 'cus you never give us candy." She looked at her sister, Katie, as if to say, "was that a good save?" The look on Katie's face said 'no.' Emma gulped. Susan looked at the girls suspiciously, but she let it go. "Okay...well dreams don't count. Don't worry, I will tell him." Emma smiled relieved. "Katie, did you like your Bionic Woman doll?" Emma was already eyeing it. "Yup, thanks, Mom...I mean, Santa." Susan didn't know if Emma still believed, or was pretending, but the two little ones certainly did, so she gave Katie a look. Katie mouthed the word 'sorry.'

A couple of years and a new apartment later, Susan knew her marriage to Al was over with. She needed to tell the girls, and she needed to do it today because she had some news to share with them. It was a few weeks after Christmas, and Susan called the girls over. "Girls, I need to talk to you." The girls were in the kitchen cleaning up after dinner, and were making up songs like they always did together. "Coming," they said in unison as they walked over to their mother. Emma was turning 10 in a couple of weeks, and Katie was turning 12 in a couple of months.

"Guess what?!" Susan was nervous and emotional. "Your dad wants to see you." Katie was surprised. She had not seen her dad in a while. She was cautious as a nearly 12-year-old, but Emma was smiling. "Really, Mom?" Emma asked excitedly. She loved her daddy, and missed him since he left for Puerto Rico. "So, he's not coming here...home?" Susan held Emma's hand. "No, Honey. We won't be married for too much longer." Emma felt sad, and looked at Katie who remained quiet.

"So yes, you get to see him, Emma. Isn't that great?" Katie was suspicious since she only heard her mother say "Emma." Susan continued; "Well the good news is you are going to see him next week, and you will take turns." Susan held her breath waiting for that to register with them. "Yay!" Emma was excited as she didn't understand what was happening, but Katie was starting to realize it. What did her mother mean by, "take turns?" "When, Mom? When? I can't wait! Does that mean we get to go to the beach?" The girls had been to Puerto Rico before, and they loved it. There they had a big family, warm weather, beaches, good food, etc. They knew they would have fun there. Katie wanted to live there from the first day that she set foot on the island.

Emma thought that this was great news, but Katie didn't look too happy. "Mom, did you say in a week?" Confusion turned into anger. She couldn't believe what she was hearing. Emma missed the part about taking turns, but Katie knew that it meant they would be separated. Susan nodded yes. "So, wait... How is this going to work?" she asked her mother. "Well," Susan replied. "We were thinking that Emma would go first with your brother, and then you the next year with your little sister, and you would all spend summers together." Susan smiled, trying to convince them that it was not a big deal, but her hands were shaking. She would miss her children.

Katie was furious. "Mom, can I talk to you for a minute?" It really wasn't a question. Katie walked into the kitchen expecting her mother to follow. Emma looked at both of them, but knew when they were this serious it was best to not get involved. Besides, she was way too excited to care. She entertained herself with her Marie Osmond doll. "Katie," Susan started, but Katie interrupted. "So, you're separating us? How could you do this?" Katie was crying. "Yes," Susan answered. "We thought it would be a good idea that you both shared your parents. You know things have been tough around here, Katie, and I need your help with the baby."

"No, Mom, please! Why do I have to stay here, why can't we all go? I want to go with Emma! You know how much I love Puerto Rico, and how close Emma and I are." Susan heard desperation in her daughter's voice, but she had to put it away somewhere deep within her. "Or better yet, why aren't we all going?" Susan was running out of patience. She didn't like feeling uncomfortable. She didn't like this either, but she felt it was necessary. She couldn't raise four kids on her own with no income. "You will understand when you are older, but for right now this is what we need to do. That's final. I wish things were better, but I need you here." "I don't think I will ever understand," Katie muttered. She ran to her room, and slammed the door. Emma looked back when she heard the door slam. She got up from playing with her brother, and went in the room the girls shared. "Katie?" Emma looked up at Katie who was on top of the bunk bed they shared. She couldn't reach so she climbed up, and sat next to her.

"What's wrong, Katie? Why are you crying?" Katie knew her sister didn't understand that they were to be separated, and her mother seemed to be in denial, so she felt it was her responsibility to make it clear to her little sis. She knew she was about to break her heart. "But, why can't you come too?" Emma sobbed. She was out of breath. "It's not fair!" Katie knew it wasn't, but they had no choice but to go with the decision their parents had made for them. Katie held Emma tight. "Emma, you will be fine with David, just make sure you take care of him like I took care of you, okay?" Emma was not happy to go with her little brother who threw his toy car at her eye, but she promised Katie that she would take care of him. "Also, you're gonna see Dad, and Grandma, and Grandpa. You can go to the beach, and there is no winter, remember?" She tried to give her hope even though she didn't have any for herself. Katie knew what she was missing by not going, and what she had to look forward to by staying. She was not happy about this at all. Susan went to check on the girls to see if they were okay, and to try to explain, but she found them sleeping side by side on the top bunk, and didn't want to wake them. She noticed the dried tears on their pretty faces, but she felt there was nothing she could do. She couldn't do this alone, and if she wasn't getting child support, then at least Al should share the responsibility.

The morning came for Emma and David to leave home, and there wasn't a dry eye in sight. The kids grabbed a few toys to take with them, and their mom packed up some of their belongings. "Don't take it all kids, you're coming back, okay?" Katie rolled her eyes and her little sister. "Emma, do you have your Marie Osmond doll?" Emma nodded. "David, do you have your favorite car?" He also nodded yes. Susan hurried the kids. "Guys, come on... the cab is outside...we have to go." Emma dropped her bag, and ran to put her shoes on. "Katie, I can't find shoes that fit, what do I wear?" Katie handed her sister a pair of sneakers that were a bit worn, grabbed her coat, and they all headed out to the cab.

The ride to the airport was quiet. Katie held her sister's hand the whole way. Once they arrived at the airport, they said their goodbyes. Emma held her mother tightly, hoping she would see her soon. Her focus right now was on seeing her dad. David, totally confused, simply held Emma's hand. Since they were travelling alone, the flight attendant assigned to their care met them outside. With a huge smile, she said "Okay you guys, are you ready to fly?" David smiled, and nodded yes. Emma was timid, and didn't answer. She handed them both an "American Airlines" pin to wear, and off they went. Katie walked back to the car, and closed the door as Susan followed. "Don't be like that, Katie. I know it's difficult, but we will get through this." Katie didn't answer. She felt that her parents had given up, and that there had to be another way to handle this situation, but she was only a kid.

A NEW FAMILY

Emma and David got on the plane with the flight attendant. She escorted them to their seats, fastened their seatbelts, and handed them a blanket and a pillow. Emma took the window seat, and helped her little brother to settle in. "Okay, David, I'm in charge now." David made a face, so she softened her voice, "...until we get to Dad's house." David smiled then, and took out some toys to play with. They had gone to Puerto Rico before, so they were excited for that, and to see their dad, but they were both confused with the separation, especially with traveling alone. Emma put her grownup self on, and felt confident without Katie for the moment.

When they arrived in Puerto Rico their dad was waiting along with their grandparents, their aunts, and some of their cousins. Emma told her brother to put on his coat because his hands were full, and they needed to carry other stuff. As soon as their grandmother saw them, she had a lot to say. "Why is David wearing a coat? Don't you know it's hot here, and why are you so skinny?" Everyone was staring at them as if they were aliens from another planet. Their dad had a great big smile on his face, and looked quite healthy...a far cry from how Emma had seen him that day at the projects. She was happy to be with him. She had missed him terribly. Everyone else in their welcoming party was probably happy to see them, but also pitied them to some degree. Grandma took over, and Emma felt like she lost all control. Even at ten years old in New York, she had some control. She and Katie would even "trick or treat" alone... so young. She got the feeling that "hanging out" was not on Grandma's mind.

They drove for what seemed like a long time, and Emma started to feel somewhat sick. She wasn't used to being in a car, and everyone spoke Spanish. She couldn't understand anything they were saying, so she stuck her head out the window for air. When they finally got to their destination, they settled into their grandparents' house which is where their dad was living.

Emma didn't mind the country. It was very different from the city she was used to, but she loved it very much. They were told to take a bath, and eat. Emma had already learned from her last trip that her grandmother was a stickler for cleanliness. Without their mother around, it appeared that their grandmother was the one in charge. Their dad also did what she said. When they were bathed and fed, their father came into their room. Emma's face lit up, but David seemed withdrawn. "How are you guys feeling? I know you miss your mom, but try to enjoy your time here now because you will be here for a long time." Emma made a face wondering what he meant by "a long time." She thought that she was supposed to see her sisters and mom during the summer, or that her mother would visit before the summer.

Al smiled at the kids not really knowing what to do next. He was used to the city, and being independent himself, so country life didn't suit him. "Dad, I missed you so much!" Emma held on to her dad for a while, and Al welcomed it. David watched, so Al turned his attention to his son. He seemed lost. "How ya' doin' Buddy?" David was going to be 7 years old next month, and Al felt like he didn't know his son very well since he had not spent very much time with him...ever. David got closer to Emma, but he smiled at his dad. "Look at my car, Daddy," he finally said. Al took the car in his hands, and complimented him on it. Emma got up, and went into the kitchen to see her grandma who was cooking, feeling that David would be okay with their dad.

"Hi, Grandma," Emma said with a smile. Grandma held her close to her, then held up Emma's arms as if she were holding up a shirt. "Let's get some food in you, Emma...you're too skinny! Don't you eat?" "I eat,

Grandma. I'm always hungry." "Well, we need to get you some shakes or something so you can gain some weight...and that hair! You need to fix yourself up, Emma." Emma, being a tomboy, and only 10 years old, didn't care much about looking girly.

A few days later when their dad came home after work, he wasn't alone. "Hey, kids." He called them over. "I want you to meet someone. This is Michelle." Emma looked at Michelle. She was pretty, clean, and smiley. David didn't seem to care too much. "Hi," Emma said shyly as she pulled David closer as if to protect him. Michelle handed something to Emma and David. Emma looked surprised. No one ever gave her gifts, except for Santa, of course. "What is it?" Emma asked. "Open it," Michelle said with a smile. Emma pulled a small black purse out of the gift bag. She knew neither Michelle nor her dad for that matter, knew her. If they did, they would have bought her a race car. She wasn't one for girly things, except for dolls. She looked at David who held up a fire truck. Secretly Emma wanted it. Her dad caught her looking at her brother, he winked at her, and she looked away. Boy, people were different here, she thought.

Emma liked Michelle, she had dark hair like her Mother and it made her feel close to her. She was kind, and put together from the tippy top of her head right down to her feet. Emma looked down at herself. She was not put together at all. She was an awkward, skinny, messy, curly haired 10-year-old who didn't have a clue about how to be girly. Her mother always did her hair, but now she was on her own, and didn't have a clue about how to do it. Emma went with the flow. The four of them spent a lot of time together, and Emma was fine with that. She just wished that Katie was also a part of it.

A few months later, their dad had some news to share. "So, Guys, we are happy you are here because now you can be part of our wedding!" Emma raised her eyebrows. "You're getting married? Aren't you already married to Mom?" It was difficult to explain to kids what divorce meant, but Al tried his best. Emma didn't feel anything. She accepted it, and moved on. Emma already liked Michelle, so to her it seemed like a good idea. David was unphased. "When, Daddy?" Emma asked. "Very soon," Al answered, holding Michelle's hand. He appeared to be happy, so Emma chose to be happy too. She was interrupted by Michelle's voice. "Emma, I want you to be the flower girl, and David, you can be the ring bearer."

Emma didn't know what that was, but she smiled anyway...it sounded good to her. She had hopes for this new family. She knew "The Brady Bunch" was happy with their new family, so she could be too.

The day of the wedding came, and it was a beautiful day. Emma got her hair done for the first time in her life, and actually looked like a put together, pretty little girl - a far cry from her tomboy self. She didn't mind it at all. The ceremony was nice, everyone sang, and the reception was a lot of fun. She had never been to a party like this. She grabbed her brother. David, look. There are fish in the water under the little bridge of the wedding cake." David stuck his finger in to touch one, and Emma slapped his hand away, giving him a look, then stuck her finger in the frosting of the cake. "Hey, not fair, Emma," he copied.

Emma really liked Michelle's family. They treated her like she was family, and now she was a real part of it. Emma especially liked Michelle's sister, Karen. She was the funniest person Emma had ever met. "Are you bringing me something from your next trip, Karen?" she asked sheepishly. She knew that every time Karen went on a trip with her agency, she would bring back cute things for David and her. "Jes," she answered, and Emma laughed. She knew she meant, "yes," but she could barely speak English. She loved that Karen would make fun of herself by singing Barry Manilow songs like "Bandstand Boogie" which was really fast, and Emma would crack up, which would then make Karen crack up. She spent a lot of that afternoon following Karen.

After the wedding, it was time for them to move into their own home. "You ready, Emma?" her dad asked. "Yes, I want to see my room." Michelle and her dad stood by as Emma opened the door to her very own bedroom. She was in awe! The twin bed sat neatly under the window, and was covered in a beautiful blanket with yellow flowers.

"Emma, do you like it?" Michelle asked. Emma walked over to her bed and moved her hand up and down the blanket as if she were actually touching the flowers. "I love it, thank you." "Now you can settle in nicely. School starts on Monday, and you can get ready in your own space." Al was proud of this moment. He hoped it would last forever.

DISAPPOINTMENTS

Emma had a difficult time in school from not knowing Spanish, so before she finished the 4th grade, her grandmother pulled her out of school. Emma wasn't happy about it since she was nearly finished. Now she would have to repeat the fourth grade, and she hated that she was already one of the older kids in her class since her birthday was in January. She was smart, and knew she could have stayed in class, but she quickly learned that anything she thought or said, didn't matter - her grandmother was in control now. David was only going into first grade, so there was no issue with him. Emma had a lot of free time now that she wasn't in school, so she spent some of it with her cousins in the city. She loved staying with them. They had such nice houses and things. Things she knew her parents couldn't offer her, but she was okay with that. Emma's cousin Clara decided to help. Clara and Emma attended the same school, so Emma would stay with her on occasion. Spending time with her cousins helped her to learn the language a lot faster, and eventually she lost the fear of reading and speaking Spanish out loud. She and David were bilingual in a matter of a few months. This was good because the new school year was about to begin.

Emma walked into her new classroom full of fourth graders. She wasn't happy about them being younger, but she had to accept it. She noticed her new school was different than the one in New York. The classroom doors and windows were open. She could go anywhere after class, even outside the school to the candy store. The teacher introduced her to the class. "Everyone, this is Emma. She is still learning Spanish, so be patient." It seemed like everyone in her class was staring at her and whispering. Mrs. Rivera walked Emma to her seat. "I love your hair, Emma, it's so long and soft." Emma smiled at her and replied. "Thank you." The kids in her class were nice to her and gave her the nickname, Gringa.

Things were looking good for Emma. She was starting to fit in, settle in, and trust again. She had a new family, her own bedroom, lots of cousins, and new friends at school. She was happy, until bad news hit their family. They lost Raquel, Michelle's sister, to an aneurysm. It was sudden and tragic. Emma was stunned. She had a special bond with Raquel. This loss was unfathomable. Emma understood loss from being separated from her mother and sisters, but she didn't know death. "Daddy, I believe Raquel is in Heaven. Do you?" Al looked at his daughter whose face was flushed from crying. "I'm sorry Emma, I know you liked her very much. Yes, I believe she is in Heaven." Al held his daughter tightly, and she continued to cry. Emma knew in her heart that she was in Heaven. Raquel was truly a good person.

Something changed in Emma when her family separated, so it was comforting for her to bond with her new family, but losing Raquel was not what she expected, and it hurt. She would make sure to be more cautious bonding with people going forward even if she seemed quiet and weird. She already felt different, so what was the big deal anyway? It's not like her family had treated her as if she was normal...only Raquel did that. Or maybe people just didn't notice her.

Emma distracted herself with her two dogs, teasing her brother, and hanging out with friends from school and the neighborhood. Things started to change at home too. She started to see a different side of Michelle, and she didn't like it. She wasn't allowed out during the week, but she had to learn that it was normal for kids to stay in when their parents weren't home. She wasn't used to not having the freedom that she had in New York, and it bothered her. Emma felt that there was more to this story.

"But Dad, why can't we go out?" Michelle interrupted, "Because we are at work, and you and your brother need to stay inside. You need to watch him. Besides, you need to clean the house, and do laundry, and don't forget the floors, and dusting the furniture. When you do the laundry, make sure to hang it up outside, pick it up when it dries, fold it all correctly, and put it all away." Michelle would yell at her if her chores weren't done, and she would yell at her if they were done incorrectly which was pretty much always. She felt like Cinderella. She was always sick with asthma so certain chores were difficult for her. Michelle didn't seem to care, nor did her dad. He didn't get involved. "David, why aren't you helping me?" He shrugged his shoulders, and simply answered, "I take out the garbage." "It's not fair!" Emma shoved him even though he wasn't the one she was upset with. She quickly apologized. "I'm sorry, David. Come on, let's play in the yard and scare someone by letting Princess loose. He shook his head no. He was mad at her for pushing him, but she knew her brother, and knew that she was the only person he trusted, so she wanted him to be happy. "How about we watch 'Mazinger?' I think it's on!" He smiled in agreement. She knew him well.

Later on, after dinner Emma was doing the dishes when she heard Michelle's voice. "Emma, what are you doing? No wonder that pan isn't clean, you're scrubbing too soft!" Emma was startled by Michelle's sudden appearance, and started to cry. She didn't feel like explaining that she had been at it for about an hour, and was doing it softly because she was tired at that point. Who would listen? She felt like she was always waiting for someone to care about her, to see how unhappy she was, for someone to save her. She also wished that she was more verbal. She hated being so shy. She was always waiting for someone to step in. Her dad let Michelle take over the disciplining, and Emma was disappointed in him for that.

One day, Emma's grandma came to visit David and her after school, and she found Emma under the bed (since she was so tiny) trying to catch every dust bunny she could find. "Emma, Honey, what are you doing under there?"

Emma heard her voice, and popped out from under the bed with her face all red, and her allergies kicking in. When she pulled herself out from under the bed, her knee landed on a piece of glass from a figurine she had broken earlier, and started bleeding. "Emma, get up...let me take a look at that?" Emma was happy to see her grandma. She knew she would have brought her some snacks. "Hi, Grandma! I was cleaning." Grandma thought her son and daughter in law, Michelle, were pushing Emma too hard. "It's okay, Honey. Let's fix that cut on your knee. I think it's pretty clean under there now." Emma got nervous she knew she would get into trouble with Michelle if she didn't finish her chores on time. "But I still have chores left to do." Grandma was not happy. She already wasn't too crazy about Michelle, and thought that she was too young for David and his kids. "It's okay...you have done enough for today." Emma knew she would hear from Michelle later, but she was obedient to her grandmother. One thing Emma prided herself on was being obedient.

Emma looked forward to the weekends. If they weren't riding their bikes, she and her brother were riding their skateboards, or skating all over the neighborhood. She needed to get all the stored-up energy out or she felt like she would explode. One of the things Emma enjoyed was terrifying the neighbors by letting out her Doberman named, Princess. She knew Princess wouldn't actually attack anyone, but she got a thrill watching everyone scramble for cover. Emma would laugh every time, and pretend it was an accident. However, one time she stopped laughing because accidentally, she let her tiny little Pomeranian, Nishka, out and she was hit by a car. Her parents, especially Michelle, were furious about it. Nishka was gone now - yet another loss. Emma cried in silence. Michelle was too busy with her own grieving, and Al was right there by her side.

As time went on, Emma and David just went with the flow. It appeared as if their lives were not their own...especially Emma's. When she finished the 6th grade they moved again. She wasn't sure if it was because they could no longer afford the rent in the city, or if her grandparents had made the decision, or both. They had moved about 7 times before she was 13 years old.

"Why are we leaving, Dad, and why can't we bring Princess with us?" Al offered some random reason why they were leaving, but at this point she knew things had changed for them. She knew he had lost his job, and could no longer afford the house they were living in. This would mean they would have to move back in with her grandparents. They had two houses out in the country, and even though she loved it there, it was far away from the city. "Emma, I thought you liked the country house?" Her dad didn't seem to understand what she was feeling. "I did Daddy, but I got used to the city and all the friends I have here. I don't want to go to another school." She knew she had no choice. They had been shifting David and her around since they arrived in Puerto Rico...yet another disappointment. Emma started to withdraw. She had lost all control of her life, and her voice. She was feeling lonely, alienated, abandoned, forgotten, neglected, and therefore, became even more distant. After all, she felt that she couldn't settle in because she never knew when the next move would be. At 13 she started the seventh grade at a new school, and created new friends. A new life yet again. At this point she wasn't surprised - it was expected. It also meant that Dad and Michelle would have to stay in the city so they could work during the week, while Emma and David lived with their grandparents. It didn't make sense to her.

"Dad, why are David and I staying here alone most of the week? Why do you and Michelle stay with her family?" "Honey, Michelle needs to be closer to her job, and I need to find a new one." Being raised by her grandparents wasn't easy because they were strict, old fashioned, and made David and her go to church about 3 to 4 times a week, which included worship rehearsal. Their grandfather was the pastor of the church, so of course, they had to attend. On the weekends when Emma's parents came home, they sometimes sang at the church. Emma loved hearing them sing. What she didn't like was that they made her join them on occasion. Emma, being terrifyingly shy, had a difficult time singing in public, but she felt like she had no choice. Everyone was constantly telling her what to do, and of course, she was "obedient."

THE PACT

Emma liked her new school. She was in junior high now, so the school was much bigger than her old one. What she liked the most was that the high school was semi-attached to her school, and the elementary school was also very near. Her brother attended that one, and she made sure to keep a close eye on him while she could also keep a close eye on the cute high school boys. She was 13 now, and ready to make new friends. She was mature beyond her years, but at the same time, very innocent, and what she wanted most in the world was to be happy. She just needed to figure out what that meant.

"Emma, I'll pick you guys up after school, okay?" Al rarely picked them up, so Emma was extremely excited to get to spend some time with her dad. When the bell rang at 3:00 PM, Emma ran ahead of everyone else. She was always running as if someone was chasing her. Her friend, Marisol yelled out, "Emma, you're going too fast...wait for me!" "HAHA, try to catch me. I'm just happy my dad is picking me up today." She ran faster, but underestimated her speed. When she tried to slow down to go down the stairs, she skipped a few steps, and fell the rest of the way on her ankle and hit her head. "Oh my gosh, Emma." Emma was in pain! She landed on her left ankle...the one she hurt as a kid on the bike. She could tell that her fall was bad because none of the kids were laughing as they hovered over her and tried to help her up.

"Wow, Mari...I really can't walk! I can't put my foot down!" She was scared and didn't like the feeling of not being able to control her body. She was in pain but didn't cry. "Emma, don't worry...you said your dad was outside, so we will help you get to him, okay? It's a good thing you weren't taking the bus today. You might need the hospital!" Emma knew she needed the Emergency Room; she didn't feel right. They walked the best they could towards the pickup line for parents. "Emma, I see him." Emma saw her dad too, and he got out of the car when he saw her being helped. "Baby, what happened?" All she needed to hear was her dad's voice, and the tears she was holding in came pouring out. She cried intensely. Her dad was here, so she would be okay now. Her friends told her dad what happened as they helped into the car. Al was worried, but instead of going to the hospital he took her home. Emma knew her dad well. He needed someone to tell him what to do, and her mom was not there to do it. She knew he was going to ask her grandparents what to do and where to go.

"Dad, I need a doctor." She couldn't stop crying. "Don't worry, you will be okay." Al looked worried. Emma was strong, a fighter, and he knew she really couldn't walk. He helped her out of the car. His parents came out to greet them, and saw that she was crying. They were worried.

"What happened?" Al explained the situation to them, and Grandma told her husband to go get help. Emma was confused. She usually would go to the hospital when she got hurt. They had her sit in a chair on the balcony until help arrived.

"Grandma, what help?" Emma was worried and in pain. "He's a family friend. He heals people. He can help you." Heals people? Emma didn't understand.

When the man arrived, they surrounded her in prayer, and then he looked at her ankle. When he touched it, she flinched. "I'm just going to see what's wrong with it, okay?" Emma let him, thinking that maybe he was a doctor, and it was his day off. As he "examined" her, she cried.

"It's not broken, but her ankle is dislocated. I can fix it." Emma's eyes widened! What was he about to do? He can fix it? Here?? What did he mean, she wondered? She held onto the chair for dear life. He grabbed her ankle, and was pressing on it, and moving it around. Emma cried harder, and her body stiffened. "No... no, please stop!" she screamed as Grandma held her. "Don't move, Honey. He is going to fix it...have faith."

Emma had faith in God, not people - she wanted him off of her foot! He continued to wiggle it around, trying to put it back together. She was screaming as he wiggled her ankle around harder and harder. Emma was confused as to what was happening. Did she not deserve the proper care? Even if it was a financial or insurance issue (which she knew it couldn't be, since every time a family member even sneezed they were in the hospital), so why not her? This was too much for her. Whatever doubts and insecurities she had, this did not help. She had other bruises on her body from the fall, but no one seemed to care, so Emma remained silent. She felt that if she spoke, and no one listened, it would hurt her even more. She hoped they would notice her outer and inner bruises. Weren't they supposed to?

"I can't seem to get it in place," the man said. Emma hated him at that moment because he wouldn't give up despite her pain. Did he not understand she was a human? It hurt her feelings that no one tried to stop him when clearly this was beyond his scope of expertise. After what seemed like an eternity, the man who she now named, "The Torturer," said he fixed it, but Emma knew he hadn't. Everyone praised God, and they let her be even though they could clearly see that she couldn't walk. "Oh, it will heal," Grandma said. Emma would walk with a limp for a long time. She hid her emotions through it all. It was a waste of time. She wondered if it was because she was Emma. She knew no one else would put their kid through anything like that. None of her cousins would ever be tortured that way. Why was she being treated differently? She felt alone.

One weekend, her parents came home after working in the city, and told the kids that Michelle was pregnant. Emma was ecstatic! She was hoping for a little sister.

"Dad, I know Grandma is in the hospital, and I hate that, but at the same time I am happy about the baby news. Emma's grandma seemed to always be in the hospital, and she didn't like that. Al understood as he had good and bad feelings as well. "I understand, Emma. I feel the same way. I am sad that Grandma is not feeling well, but thank God for good news. We needed a little of that, didn't we?" "Yup! We sure did!"

She noticed the look of worry on her father's face. "What happened to her this time?" "It's her heart, Honey, but she is in good hands, and all we can do is pray for her." She agreed she would pray for her grandmother.

"Michelle and I are going to visit her tomorrow in the city, so you and David need to stay here with Grandpa. You guys have school, and he needs the company." Emma was saddened. She loved her grandma even though she was strict, and knew that David was her favorite. She taught her how to sew, and how to be a lady. Grandma was not too keen on Emma's tomboyishness. She did love how feminine her grandmother was, even though she wasn't so herself. Once in a while she would try on her jewelry, and her favorite face powder from Maja. She had become her mother in a sense. Emma loved her grandparents, but she had to admit that her grandpa was a lot easier, so she did not mind one bit staying home with him. He was a pastor, and a very kind and loving man.

"Tell Grandma we love her," she told her dad. "I will, and make sure to keep an eye on Grandpa. You know how to use the nebulizer, so make sure that if he needs it, you help him." She waved goodbye to her dad.

Grandpa stayed behind to tend to Emma and David since they had school. He was already in the kitchen making dinner. She loved her grandparent's cooking, and she loved that there was always food and snacks. She and David ate and drank whatever they wanted when they were there.

"Bendición, Abuelo," she said to him. "Dios te bendiga, Hija," he replied. "Thanks for helping me, Emma." She gave him a sweet smile and said, "Oh, you're welcome, Grandpa." They kept each other company. Grandpa was the calm one. Sometimes it felt as if they were taking a vacation from Grandma's constant rants, but they loved her still. After they ate, the kids went to their room to get ready for school the next day, and for bed. "Kids, don't forget to read your prayer devotional before bed, okay?" he yelled out. "We won't," they replied.

Emma went to David's room to hang out for a bit, but she really wanted to find out how he was doing in school. "David...everything okay at school?" She heard a rumor that someone was bothering him, so she wanted to see if he would tell her. She loved David, and wanted to protect him. She might not have had a voice of her own, but she developed one for him. He was a cute, innocent, studious, and socially awkward boy.

She couldn't stand it when people ignored him or teased him. He didn't answer, but just looked at her. "You know, if anyone bothers you just come to me, okay?" He nodded yes, but looked lost in a way almost like he needed something. She knew that if she was feeling lost, that had to be what he was feeling too. She just didn't know what to do since she was only 13 years old herself.

When she got to her room, she closed the door and grabbed her daily devotional book to read. She never forgot to give thanks and pray - even though she didn't have a full understanding of what it meant to do that. After all she'd been through, she questioned whether or not God cared. She just thought that maybe He was busy with people who really needed him.

Emma heard a light knock on her door. "Emma." It was her grandfather. "Come in, Grandpa." With a smile she said, "Look see, I'm reading my prayer devotional." Her grandpa smiled back at her. "Yes, I can see...very good. God is happy with you. I have a gift for you, Emma." She looked at him and felt...boy, did she love this man. He was everything anyone could want in a grandpa, and the only person who seemed to care about her. "Oh, thank you, Grandpa. Why? It's not my birthday." He handed her a JC Penney bag that had a little box with a ribbon on it. She was excited. "Just a little something for you for helping me when I am sick," he said smiling. "Aw, thanks, Grandpa!" She took the box out of the bag, removed the ribbon and wrapper, and stared at it. She was surprised. She didn't have to open the actual box since it had a clear plastic top. What she saw really confused her. She looked at her grandfather, and saw him smiling as she held a little box of sexy, lacy black and red underwear. She never wore underwear like that before, nor had even seen any.

"Do you like them?" Without waiting for her answer he said, "Pull them out so you can see better." She was confused and now uncomfortable since he usually just checked on them and went to bed. "Come on...open them up!" He was persistent and seemed quite different to her. "Um, okay," she replied as she pulled one out. She thought they were pretty, but certainly not for her. "They're pretty, Grandpa. Thank you." She quickly put them back in the box... her hand shaking. "Try them on...let's see if they fit. I wasn't sure of your size." Emma didn't feel comfortable at all, and wanted him to leave. "I will try them on tomorrow, thank you, Grandpa," she replied, and didn't understand why he would buy her something so personal. She wondered if her grandma wore them, but for some reason she didn't think so. Grandpa insisted she try them on right there and then. He wasn't going to leave the room. "Try them on now, because if they don't fit, I have to return them." Something in his voice shook her to the core.

She was nervous, and wondered if God could see how he was behaving. She grabbed the black one, and got up to walk towards the bathroom, but her grandfather grabbed her hand and made her stay. "Right here is fine, Honey. Don't worry, it's just me." She wondered now if he was ever even sick, or if he just wanted to be alone with her. She looked at the door, hoping that her brother would walk in, but she knew he was sleeping. She decided not to think anything bad since this was the one adult she truly trusted. He was kind, loving, generous, and her Pastor. Everyone respected him, and loved him. At the same time, she had never felt this kind of fear or confusion before. She believed in him...nothing would happen...how could it? Her mind was playing tricks on her, and her heart was beating out of her chest.

Before she made the next move to try them on, he grabbed her, and touched her. She was shocked, and began to cry out loud. She pushed him away, and asked him to stop in between sobs. He wouldn't! He betrayed her! Didn't he see that she was just a kid? Didn't he care that she was his own granddaughter? She didn't know what was happening. She felt lost, used, confused, hurt, and every bad feeling under the sun. She allowed her mind to leave her body. Her asthma kicked in, and her heart felt like it would explode.

She wasn't sure how long he had stayed in her room, but she was relieved when he finally left. He simply told her that she was beautiful, turned off the light, and walked out. She cried all night, and could hardly breathe. Every hour that night, the man who was once her trusted grandfather would come into her room to check on her.

Even though she didn't sleep that night, she couldn't wait to get to school to feel normal again. She pretended that nothing had happened, and from that day on, she carried the weight of his impending death on her shoulders since he told her that he would die if the pact wasn't finished. She could not tell anyone about what happened or what would continue to happen to her. He said that he would die if she told anyone about it.

At school, although happy to be away from home, she felt like she was walking on a cloud of troubled winds. She had no idea what to do about how she was feeling. She knew that something bad had happened to her, but she couldn't accept it emotionally, so she put it away somewhere deep, and told no one. He was the one person who she would have told because he was the only person she trusted and respected, being her Pastor and all.

After school he picked up David and her. Grandfather kept looking at her as they drove in silence. She was in the front seat, and thought it was over until he put his hand on her leg. When they got home, he had made them something to eat, and he called her into the kitchen to talk to her. He repeated what he said the night before.

"Emma, this is a pact with God, and you can't tell anyone. I am blessing you with prayer and anointing. We have to stick together on this so it will work. God will protect you from anyone harming you and your body. If you don't listen to me, God said I can die from a heart attack!" Emma knew he was speaking, but only heard the manipulating words about "a pact with God," and something about dying. She was already feeling alone, abandoned, and neglected in her life. She certainly did not need this experience. This was on a completely different level. She had never heard about something like this happening between a child and an adult. She wondered what she had done wrong to deserve this. God was confusing her...she thought that her grandfather was a good man. She could no longer pray or trust church people. Only once in a while would she lift her head up to the sky and ask, "Why?" She believed in God, but didn't understand what his role in her life was.

"God, why?!" she asked out loud. "Do you not love me? No one else does - I thought you did, God? What pact is this? Why was I chosen? I behave, I pray, I do well in school, I am obedient and quiet, so why God?" She wept.

She felt broken, and didn't know how she would survive this. Being at school helped since she was never allowed out, or allowed to attend school trips or outings. At least she could be a young girl at school, and boys liked her, but she didn't trust them. As time went on, the "pact" was not fulfilled yet because her grandfather continued with his sinister behavior towards her, and she felt like she was losing more of herself each time.

"Emma," Michelle called to her. "Yeah, Michelle." She hoped that maybe she had found out, and would save her. "Grandpa wants to pray for you, and asked me for permission, so of course, I said he could, okay?" Emma was shocked at hearing this. "What?" "He doesn't want you to get sick, so he wants to pray over your body?"

Emma couldn't believe what she was hearing. Did Michelle not realize what he was doing? "Over my body?" she asked her. She couldn't believe that Michelle could have possibly heard Grandfather correctly. "Yes, your body. He said that he needed to pray for your, um, private areas. He said that he felt you were going to get sick, and he needed to bless you with oil." Yup, Emma thought. She heard right, but didn't get it...Wow! How could she allow that?

"I'll be right outside the bedroom, okay?" as if that would help, Emma thought. Her soul ached. "Could this be right?" she wondered. If other adults were involved, the pact was real? She felt hopeless. "Um, okay, Michelle, if you think he should." This meant that Grandfather would find a way to molest her even when family members were around.

Emma learned how to bottle up her emotions. She was used to it after all. The only time she would let her aggressions out was when her brother was getting picked on at school by bullies, like the day her friends ran up to her and shouted, "Emma, it's your brother...hurry - someone is beating him up!" Emma ran following her friends. She got to the spot where her brother, David was getting beaten up. "Oh, not today boys!" she said under her breath. Filled with anger, she jumped on the other boys, pulling them off her brother one by one, while punching them, and pulling their hair. She knew her brother's angry outbursts, and he was having one now. He just didn't know where to guide it.

"You jerk! Get off my brother! You fight against one kid?!" Emma yelled while pulling their hair, and hitting them as hard as she could. Both boys backed off, and apologized to her. She walked away with her friends and brother to calm him down. "David, what is wrong with you? Why do you get yourself in these situations?" He was crying, but mostly out of anger. Then she held his hand, and made him look at her.

"David, I told you to come to me. Don't let anyone push you around. I love you, okay?" He was crying. "They wouldn't talk to me, Emma." She was furious that he would even want them to. One thing about Emma was that she was not a follower. If she didn't have strength to fight off the adults in her life, she certainly did have the strength to not care about what kids said about her. She wasn't popular because she didn't want to be. All she needed was herself, a couple of good friends, and her brother to stay out of trouble.

Emma had to break up a few fights for her brother, but never had one of her own. She knew she had to keep 'secrets' because she needed to keep it together for David. A few weeks later, her parents and her grandma were at home. Emma felt relieved. She went to the bathroom to wash her hands, and when she walked out, she saw her grandfather sitting on his bed calling her to come near. She shook her head no, and pointed to the living room. He knew that everyone was home, so what was he doing? She walked towards her grandmother's bedroom to get one of her magazines. She always had the newest "VEA," and "Teve Guía" from her aunt's pharmacy. She looked at all of her grandmother's things in her bedroom like she always did. "Why doesn't Grandpa love me anymore?" She felt great sadness.

She heard her grandfather call her again, and walked half way over to him so that he would shut up. "Kiss me!" She got so nervous. "What? Dad is here...no!" "It's okay... kiss me quick! They won't see." She continued to refuse. If she was caught, she would die of embarrassment. He said it again, and when she again shook her head 'no,' something happened.

"Dad!" Emma screamed as her parents ran over to where she was. When they walked in the room, they saw Grandfather on the floor seizing, and vomiting at the same time. "Call an ambulance," Al yelled out.

Emma stood in a corner of the room paralyzed. "I caused this," she thought. "I didn't kiss him, and now he had a heart attack." Emma was beside herself. He was telling the truth, and his life depended on her. She was horrified! The ambulance came, and their trip to the city was cancelled...they were all off to the hospital.

"Emma," her dad called to her as he came out of his father's hospital room. She looked up. "Grandpa wants to see you, and don't worry, he is doing a lot better thanks to you. It is a good thing that you saw him when you did." Emma did not want to see him. Hesitantly, she walked towards his room. He had an oxygen mask, and wires everywhere. "Emma," he said in a raspy voice and out of breath. "You see what happened? I told you to kiss me." Emma cried and felt that her life was over. She would have to comply.

THE LITTLE HOUSE ON THE PRAIRIE

Some months later, Emma dealt with her grandfather over and over again, but she put it away in some place where she didn't feel emotion...somewhere deep, away from everyone. She was too focused on Katie's upcoming visit... the first since her own arrival three years ago.

"Did it get here yet, Dad?" Emma kept looking at her watch. "It looks like they landed. We just have to wait for her to come down the stairs... be patient."

Emma couldn't wait. She felt like she did when she waited for the yellow school bus when her sister came home from school. This time she was coming to visit her in Puerto Rico. Although she would have liked to see her mother and little sister too after three years waiting, she knew that would happen one day. Just like that, Katie's pretty face showed up in a crowd of people.

"There she is!" Emma yelled over to her dad. "Come on, David, let's go see Katie." David followed his sister. His memories of Katie were few, but he did have some good ones of her. When Katie saw everyone, she had a great big smile on her face. She dropped her bag, and ran over to her dad, but Emma jumped in front before Katie got to him.

"Me first!" Emma grabbed her sister and held on tightly...she felt safe. Katie was only two years older than Emma, but appeared to be a lot older. S he had the most amazing green eyes and red lipstick, that their grandmother was not too happy about. "You are too young for lipstick, Katie!" Katie laughed.

"Grandma, I just got here." She was not about to let anyone control her. Emma wished she could be more like her. She loved her free spirit.

"Katie, are you staying to live with us?" Emma asked hopefully. Katie smiled as she hugged her. "We will talk about that later, but for now, I am staying. I don't really want to go back to New York, but we will see." That's all Emma needed to hear, so she held her hand behind her back, and crossed her fingers.

Back at the country home they were living in now, Katie looked around, and you could tell that this was not her thing. Emma noticed that her sister took a very deep breath and closed her eyes.

"Well, one thing is for sure - the air is better here." Her dad laughed. "Katie, I'm glad you're here. Next week, you will be signed up for school, and we can hang out together. Emma knew that for now, Katie was staying for a few months, so she needed to go to school, and this made her happy.

A week later Al dropped his three kids off at school. "Let's go, Katie!" When they walked into the hallway, all eyes were on Katie. Emma felt proud. Her sister was the new shiny toy, and beautiful at that. All the boys wanted to date her, and all the girls wanted to be her. She was confident, social, and beautiful while Emma (although she was liked by a lot of boys too), was skinny, wore no makeup, and dressed in whatever clothes her grandmother bought for her. She had friends, but wasn't too popular, although having a sister like Katie suddenly made her more popular - at least for the time being.

"Katie, are you coming to church with us tonight?" Emma knew Katie was not keen on going to church, and even though Emma had to do whatever her parents and grandparents told her, Katie seemed to be exempt. She did what she wanted to do most of the time. She was used to her freedom, and not having so many family members, or rules, or church in her life. She began to refer to their life in the country as living in an episode of "The Little House on the Prairie."

"Not tonight...you guys go too much, Emma." Emma smiled, and replied, "Okay, see you later, Sis." Emma had something up her sleeve for after church, and she was about to drag her brother into it. After the service, Emma and David ran ahead of their parents. Their church was right up the block within walking distance. "Dad, I'm going ahead." He waved at her giving his approval. "David, let's scare Katie!" David was totally on board. Since they lived in the country, the house and its surroundings were not very visible from the road. She knew Katie would freak out if she heard noises. When they reached the house, they began their scare tactic.

"David you go to that side of the house, and start banging on the windows, and I'll go to the other side." He agreed, and they both took their assigned places. Without a word they started to bang on the windows, and scratch the tin covers. Katie and David laughed when they heard Katie freaking out. "Who's there?" Her voice cracked as she shouted out, "Hello?" She peeked through a window, and the kids ducked.

"Hey what are you guys doing?" Emma and David heard their dad, so they ran to the front of the house. "Nothing," Emma said as she elbowed David. "Nothing," he also replied. Then Al heard Katie's nervous voice. "Dad?" "Yeah, Honey, it's us." She opened the door slowly, and they found her holding a machete, a small knife, and her dad's BB rifle. The kids laughed so hard they had tears in their eyes.

"Honey, what are you doing?" Al asked his obviously frightened daughter. She had tears in her eyes. "I heard some noises, Dad...I'm scared." Al turned to look at the very guilty two other kids. "What?!" Emma asked but couldn't contain her laughter. Katie dropped the weapons. "It was you guys? Are you kidding me?" Al couldn't help but laugh also, and Michelle hugged Katie. "Guys, why would you do that? It's not nice." "No, it isn't," Katie chimed in. "Just another day at 'The Little House on the Prairie,'" Emma sarcastically said. "Fine!" Katie answered. "Maybe I'll go to church next time." Emma winked at David.

All was well in Emma's world with her sister now home, but she still never told her "the dirty little secret" she was keeping. A few weeks later, things were different. Katie was beginning to feel controlled...like she was losing the freedom she was accustomed to. "Katie, the freedom you have had is not normal for a 15 year-old. Even though I know you are used to it, it's not what we allow here." They were constantly going at it like that, because Katie tried to fight for Emma's freedom as well. "She's only 13 years old, Katie." "Yes, but you keep her locked up like she's a prisoner! She can't do anything, or go anywhere!" She didn't get it, and Al was not giving in.

A few days later the kids were in the kitchen eating when all of a sudden, their dad walked in very slowly backwards, pulling a bag across the floor like it was very heavy. Michelle followed behind holding his BB rifle. The kids looked at them, and stood up feeling nervous. Katie jumped up on a chair. "What are you doing to my dad, Michelle?" Michelle looked nervous, and didn't understand what Katie was asking. Al stepped in. "Guys please, give us some room here, we have to do something - step back!" Now they were really nervous. Katie looked scared, like she was about to witness a murder. Emma and David looked just as confused.

Suddenly Al shook the bag, and out came a foot and a half long centipede! They all screamed and ran further into the kitchen. Al grabbed the BB gun, and instead of shooting it (which wouldn't have made much sense), poked it with the edge. "Oh, my gosh, Dad! All the guts are coming out," Emma shrieked. David moved in closer to check it out. Michelle looked relieved.

"That was so scary," she said. "I was changing into my pajamas when that thing came towards me." Al threw it outside into the woods, and closed the door. He noticed Katie crying. He dropped the bag, and ran to her. "Honey, what's wrong?" Al asked his daughter who was as pale as a ghost. "I thought Michelle was gonna kill you." Everyone laughed.

Emma was having a blast making fun of her sister being a city girl, and she knew that her visit would not be a long one. She was not accustomed to living in the country or being raised as strictly like Emma was. She hated it.

It didn't take long before Katie had had enough. She missed New York too much. Emma understood and was grateful for the three months she had with her, but she was heartbroken. She had hoped her sister would fall in love with Puerto Rico just like she did. "I don't want you to leave, Katie." Katie gave her a warm hug.

"Emma, maybe you can come to New York soon." Emma smiled, and hoped that she would go one day soon to see her mom and little sister...it had been three years.

THE BIG REVEAL

Emma felt lost when her sister left. Her parents were oblivious to what was happening to her, and no one noticed that there was something wrong in her life. Grandfather had stepped away from her a little when Katie was there like perhaps he knew better. Emma still suffered inside, and it started to show on the outside. She was skinny, sick all the time, and wasn't doing great in school. Why didn't anyone notice, she wondered?

"Emma, you're too 'flaca.' I'm going to buy you vanilla shakes to fatten you up again." Emma would just nod, but what she was really thinking was, "Grandma don't you see what's happening? Don't you see what your husband is doing to me?" Those thoughts were blocked by witnessing the heart attack he had suffered because of her.

Michelle approached Emma. She had calmed down about all the chores since they moved. "Emma, guess what?" Michelle asked excitedly. "We are having a baby!" She was beaming. "Finally, some good news," Emma thought. "Yes! I'm so happy. Yay!" Emma felt happy for the first time in years. She would take care of this baby. She would make sure no one hurt it - this was her special surprise. Thank you, God. Emma gave thanks. This little girl could brighten anyone's day, and she was exactly what Emma needed especially now that she was 14 years old, and had gone through so much.

When the baby was born, they named her after Michelle's sister, Raquel who had died. Emma was thrilled that it was a girl! She finally had a sister who actually lived with her. David didn't care much as he was too busy figuring out what was happening in his own life, and dealing with the bullies at school which kept Emma distracted since she was used to fighting them off for him.

This new baby girl made Emma feel special since she had become a loner, and her dad was changing again...going back to his old self. It was a slow process, but she noticed. She had learned at a young age that addiction was tough to fight, so Emma prayed every night for her dad. She needed something stable, and for the first time in her life she felt that Raquel was it - she held onto her for dear life.

"I will watch her Michelle. You can go with Dad." Emma volunteered to watch Raquel as much as she could. It was a distraction, and also kept Grandfather away...at least she hoped that it would. But Grandfather didn't stop. It took a year of Emma's life for her to almost lose herself, her innocence, and her sanity before she shared the terrible secret with anyone. Once in a while she would ask God why, and wait for Him to answer her.

"Okay, Emma, so tonight you stay at Grandpa's because he's sick, and you know how to use the asthma machine. You know that Grandma is in the hospital again." She looked pleadingly at her dad as she tried to enter his mind so he could see what was happening, but he couldn't.

Emma went to brush her teeth as Michelle was getting ready in the bathroom. She kept looking at Michelle, to see if she maybe could read her mind. "So, Emma, take David with you if you want. We will see you in the morning, okay?" Emma looked at her intensely, and didn't answer. "Why can't she read my mind. God, please, I can't see him today...I can't! Please no more, God!" At that moment, tears welled up in her eyes. "Emma?" Michelle didn't understand why she was crying. "Emma, what's wrong?"

"I don't want to go to my grandfather's house," she said crying. "Oh, it's okay, do you have a headache?" Emma felt her body tremble.

It looks like the truth was about to come out. She couldn't hold it in if she tried. Right then, she cried uncontrollably, and started shaking terribly. Michelle became very nervous, and dropped her moisturizer. "Emma!

What's the matter?! Emma, tell me right now!" Emma could not catch her breath as she tried to speak, so she pointed to her body, and Michelle's eyes widened.

"Emma, is Grandpa hurting you?!!" It was the first time that Emma had heard, and felt a sense of assertiveness from Michelle. Emma nodded yes. "He touches me." Michelle began to cry, and held Emma close to her. "Oh, Emma! Oh, my God, he's in love with you! How can this be? Oh, Honey, I'm so sorry. Why is he doing this? I trusted him! Emma, please listen...he will never hurt you again, I promise...it's over!" She held Emma tight, and for the first time in years, Emma felt safe. She felt her heart soften for Michelle, because she believed her...no questions asked.

"I am so sorry, Emma. I am so stupid. I am so sorry. How could I let him manipulate me like that?" she said with tears welling up in her eyes.. "We have to tell your father...we have to move...we have to do something!" She saw Michelle thinking, freaking out, blaming herself, and trying to come up with a solution for this huge problem. Somehow, Emma wasn't so sure that Michelle would have the support that she would need to deal with this sort of thing. But one thing was for sure... Emma knew that Grandfather would never hurt her again.

Her dad heard the news that seemed to swim in his brain, and not land anywhere. He didn't seem to grasp the severity, or he didn't know what to do with the news - Emma couldn't tell.

"Al, did you hear me? We have to move! We can't let the kids live here." In slow motion, Al nodded yes. He hugged Emma, but she felt that he was distant...not distant from her, but from himself. He couldn't summon the courage to look at her. Emma could see the guilt and hopelessness in his face. He was numb and ashamed of what his father had done to his daughter. Emma looked at her dad, and didn't say it out loud, but she thought that she needed him to be her superhero, and fix this - it seemed impossible.

Everything after that stayed the same, except Grandpa never hurt her again which Emma felt was good enough. "What did people do when something like this happened with a family member?" Emma questioned in her mind. A few days later they were at Emma's aunt's house. Grandma, her parents, and two of her aunts were in her aunt's bedroom for a family meeting. Michelle thought they should all know...Emma agreed. Emma was watching TV with her cousins. Grandfather was sitting with the children as well since he was not included in the "meeting."

Emma knew that the meeting was about him, but she wasn't sure why he was not in it. "What's happening in there, Emma?" he asked her. Emma shrugged her shoulders, and moved away from him. Grandfather appeared to be getting nervous. Emma felt good that there was a family meeting because she felt like she deserved some justice. This was a serious matter. After a while, they called Grandfather in. Until that moment, he did not know that Emma had told the truth.

Emma saw Michelle and her dad leave the room. "Let's go, we are leaving." Until they found a place of their own, they were going to live in her grandparents' city apartment which she believed had belonged to her aunt." Emma got up to leave, but was waiting for her grandma and aunts to come out and talk to her. "Aren't they going to call me in too?" Michelle looked at her and nodded, no. "What? Well, what did Grandma say? I don't want her to be sad. Does she still love me? What about my aunts... do they blame me?" She had all these questions that she somehow knew must have an answer.

As some time went on, Emma noticed that she didn't see her family as much as she did before. She would stay with her cousins on occasion, but everyone kept her dad at a distance. She thought it might be due to his past, but she knew there was more to it. She felt in her heart that her dad needed help...maybe her aunts, and her Grandma too. He was their father and husband after all, but mostly she needed help.

"Michelle, thank you for believing in me. I'm glad that I have you in my life. I wish my family would say something to me. I don't understand why they ignore me." Michelle hugged her. "I blame myself, but thank you for that." When they got home, Michelle told Emma that her dad wanted to talk with her, so she went to her room, and waited. When he walked in, he looked defeated.

"Emma..." Emma paused before answering, "Yeah, Dad?" He looked so nervous. "Um, I just wanted to say that you are going to be okay. Dad is never going to bother you again. He knows that you know, and he is sorry. I'm sorry too, Emma." Emma was just happy that it was over. She wanted to hear more from her dad, like something about moving, but he didn't say it.

"Okay, Dad." She felt unwanted, as if what happened was her fault, and she was a nuisance. She was left to deal with her feelings alone. It was evident that every adult just wanted "it" to go away. It was swept under the rug, and never talked about again. Emma felt like she needed to talk about it...she needed help.

"Well is it my fault, Michelle? Why won't anyone talk to me about it? Why won't anyone tell me everything is going to be okay, and they have my back?" She felt like her grandfather got away with it. Whose side was everyone on...a pedophile's? "Why did they protect him, Michelle?" She felt betrayed! Emma cried, and so did Michelle.

"Honey, it was not your fault. I should have known, and I will live with this guilt for the rest of my life. He let the devil use him, and I allowed it too." Emma was puzzled and said, "No, you are the only one who believed me, and talked to me about it." But Michelle knew the signs were there. "Why had she not seen it?" she asked herself. "And Dad is being weird...he doesn't come home sometimes. He used to do that when I was little. Why is he doing this again? Is it because of what happened to me?" Michelle couldn't answer, but it seemed logical that Al's knowledge about his own father molesting his own daughter would trigger old feelings of incompetence. Michelle needed to address it with her husband.

"Al, we have to do something. We can't live here near them anymore. It is not healthy for Emma." Al knew it was true. "I know, Michelle. We will move...we will do something, okay?" Michelle knew his words could not be taken at face value. She didn't feel that she was being supported by him, or by anyone else.

"So, do I still have to be around him? Is he going to take us, and pick us up from school?" Michelle understood what Emma was saying, but she also did not know how to handle something like this, especially when no one had her back. She chose to pray for her every day, and knew there would be justice someday. After school one day that week, Grandfather asked to speak to Emma. She didn't want to, but her parents told her that she had the right to an apology, and they would be there to witness it.

Her grandfather was in the living room with her father when he called her in. Michelle held her hand, and walked with her. "It's okay, Emma, we are here with you." She kept her distance as she listened to her grandfather speak.

"I am, Emma..." He seemed to be very nervous...Emma noticed. She didn't care. She no longer believed anything he said anyway. "I listened to the devil. I gave in to temptation. I am so sorry." Emma wondered why he was tempted to begin with. How can anyone ever be tempted by a kid and family? She didn't understand it. She had never heard of anything like this, nor did anyone ever warn her. He had a letter in his hand, and he handed it to her. She didn't take it, so Michelle took it instead, and they left the room.

"Do you want me to read it?" Emma shook her head, and looked at the paper in Michelle's hand. She didn't say anything as she took the letter, and locked herself in the bathroom. When Emma was done reading the letter from her grandfather, she handed it to Michelle. "Michelle, please keep it with you. I don't want to ever see it again."

As Emma got older, she did okay, but not really great in school. Her parents never told her that she needed to perform well in school, nor did they ask how school was, so it was never something she thought about. She also never thought about setting a goal for her future. While she was a junior in high school, her parents told her that they were moving back to the city. She was happy that she would not be near her grandfather, but knew that she would miss her friends.

"So what if I'm the new girl again? David, how do you feel about it?" Somehow she knew he would be happy. Her brother needed a change from all the bullying he was enduring.

"Yup, I'm good with it too. Are you okay though? I mean you are almost a senior." The thought of being a senior, a high school graduate, and prom never occurred to Emma. She never talked about it with her friends. Maybe the new school would be different.

"Yeah, I'm okay with moving now. I'm surprised that you even thought about it, David." Her brother was growing up too, she thought as they smiled at each other.

Being the "shiny new thing" was fun for Emma. What else was she going to do? God only knew... she moved a million times...she didn't care, so the move didn't affect her much. She enjoyed the fact that kids didn't know anything about her. It didn't matter to her like it did to other girls - to have popularity, friends, and parties - it just wasn't her scene. She was never a follower, and didn't intend on becoming one now.

"Dad, I like it here. I'm glad we are back in the city." Al was pleased to hear it. He finally felt like he had done something right. Emma continued, "You know what I was thinking? Life is like a road with many curves and turns, and all we can do is try to follow it the best we can, hoping that when we reach the end all those curves and turns were worth it." Al thought about what Emma said, and knew that she was right...especially since he was the one who chose so many wrong curves and turns.

Emma's high school classes started early, and they ended early. The building was shared with the local middle school, so when Emma finished school at about 12:30, it was time for her brother to go in until 3:30. While her parents were at work, David would stay with little Raquel until Emma got home, and she would then take over. When David got home from school, Emma was in charge of them both. It was not easy for her... she just did it.

"Why do I always have to babysit? I want to just do things in my room alone," she asked her parents, but they simply expected her to do it while at the same time, maintain the household and do the cooking. Although Emma and Michelle were on better terms now, she was still annoyed with her, especially with how she treated her brother. She was always on him, yelling and hitting him. Emma always intervened because her dad did nothing about it. It was hard on Emma, but again, no one seemed to care.

She took to writing more, journaling her feelings, and venting on paper...it helped. She also was into pen pals, and writing to her friends from her old school because she had no social life here. Taking care of the kids was too much for her, and she ended up having a breakdown one day. No one noticed it as she kept it to herself, but she locked herself in her room and just screamed into a pillow. What else could she do? This was not the life she asked for, and although she was willing to chip in since it was her home too, everything just became too much for her. She lost her voice a long time ago, and had yet to get it back.

One day, her focus shifted. She met a boy, and he was one of the cutest and most popular boys in school. She was extremely shy. It was like her insecurities had overcome her since no one ever cared about her feelings, thoughts or opinions, so she stopped talking altogether.

The only person she could talk to and laugh with was her brother, David. She could be herself with him, but with everyone else she was emotionless and voiceless...especially now that they had moved. . .again. The students were nice, but being so shy and closed-in didn't help her to make friends easily. She felt like she was more mature than they were...like she had already lived a lifetime.

"Dad, these kids are so.... 'smiley,' and 'bright eyed!' What is that about?" Al didn't know how to answer since he had not been too happy in his life either.

"Just be yourself, Honey. You are special, and you will make friends." Emma loved her dad...he had such a caring heart.

Addiction must be so difficult she thought. She knew something was up with her family. They didn't seem to be happy anymore. Al started to disappear again. She learned that it was what he did when he didn't know how to handle something in his life. It was hard on Michelle, but especially on the kids. Emma knew she needed to have a chat with her little brother.

"David, I am here for you and baby Raquel...we are in this together. We will be okay, because I am going to protect you. I love you guys." Baby Raquel didn't understand, but cried sensing that her big sister was sad. David trusted his sister to the fullest...more than anyone else he knew.

Emma, trying to keep her sanity, did what she knew best. She woke up every morning, and went to school. She never heard a word from her parents or anyone else to do well in school, to try, to focus on graduation, SAT's and college. She heard the kids at school talk about it, but it seemed so out of her reach that she didn't want to get involved. The only person that seemed to care about her was her grandfather. He didn't hurt her anymore, but his occasional presence took its toll. She wondered why she still had to be around a child molester. Was there no punishment? Did no one care, or realize how much being around him at family functions or visits bothered her? It was as if no one noticed her existence except him, until that one day - the cutest boy passed her in the hallway, and called her "Pretty Eyes."

PRETTY EYES

He called her "Pretty Eyes." Emma turned around to see the handsome boy who was speaking to her. He would call her that every time he saw her. She would blush, and be paralyzed. Her head was spinning with this new feeling, and she felt her heart beating loudly in her chest. "Can I speak to you?" he asked. She screamed, "YES!" in her mind, but in real time she simply nodded.

"Do you have a boyfriend?" Emma looked at him suspiciously. "How could he think that?" she wondered. Has he taken a good look at her? She's almost invisible to the world. At least, that's what she thought. She shook her head "no" to the most handsome surfer boy with his beach-tan skin, beautiful smile, and green eyes.

"Okay," he responded as he gave her a big smile, and walked away. "That's it?" she asked herself. She grinned and hoped he would talk to her again. As it turns out, he surely did. Every day he would look for her or randomly walk into her class. The teachers knew him and would just say, "Okay, Kyle talk to your friends later." He would always wink at Emma on the way out. She loved it, but would never show him. "Emma, why are you so shy?" she would wonder... she hated it.

"Hey Emma...what's up? What are you up to?" asked a different boy that she knew. He was from NY too, but she looked around for the cute surfer. "Oh hey, Pete." He was in love with her, and she knew it. She tried to keep her distance because of it.

"I got you some chocolate." Her eyes opened wide at the box of chocolates. He wasn't kidding. "Um, thank you, Pete, Why?" She wondered why she wasn't shy with him. "Just because...enjoy them, okay?" He left and she was still looking around school for Kyle. "Emma,why are you looking for him? It's not like you are going to say anything to him?" she asked herself. She walked across the street to get a soda at the store, and when she turned around after paying for it there stood the tall, handsome, nicely tanned boy with the most amazing green eyes. His smile could light up a room! He always looked happy. She hoped he truly was, and also hoped that it was because he saw her.

"Hi, Pretty Eyes," he said as he smiled at her. She didn't smile back, but looked down and tried to pass by him, but he blocked her way. "Hi," she said with a monotone voice. "Ugh, Emma what is wrong with you? Speak!" But she couldn't...all she could say was "Hi." He moved over so she could pass by. "Bye," he said, and she could barely walk.

"Why are my legs shaking? This is so embarrassing," she thought. The next day she woke up nice and early, and arrived at school excited and ready to see Kyle. When she got out of her first class, she saw him on the stairs hanging out, looking cute, and he waved to her as he made his way towards her. She thinks she smiled at him, but that interaction was interrupted by Pete standing in her face.

"Hey, Emma. Let's hang out." She was so annoyed when Kyle turned around and left. "Ugh! What do you want Pete?" "Nothing...just wanted to say hi, and give you this CD. You should listen to it." He left, but she noticed that he looked over at Kyle. Pete had caught on and realized that Emma had another admirer, and he was competing. Emma was upset. Instead of Pete being a friend to her, he was jealous and would do things to annoy Kyle on purpose.

The next day, while Emma waited for her next class, she saw Kyle walking towards her. She smiled within and hoped that she would be able to say a word or two. "Hey Emma, how are you feeling today?" Out of nowhere, Pete popped up again and he blocked her view of Kyle. When she turned her head to the side to see Kyle, he was walking away from them. That's it! Emma had enough. "Pete, why do you always bother me? Leave me alone, okay? I don't like you. Just stop!" She was furious until she saw Pete's face. "Fine, you don't have to be so mean. Bye!" She was still mad, but felt bad about how she dissed him. She had never done that before, but why didn't he see that she really didn't like him...or did he? She couldn't worry about it right now. She knew that she never gave him an indication that she was interested, and she was pretty obvious about liking the surfer boy.

As time went on, Kyle and Emma started dating. She was a girl of few words and he was a boy of many. He liked that she was shy. He knew that she was a good person, and that soon enough she would trust him. He made her feel comfortable. Kyle was romantic and affectionate...something Emma needed desperately since she never knew love and hoped that this was it. She loved his heart. He was kind and caring, but also a tough kid...she liked that about him. Rough around the edges and talented. He surprised her at every turn. He surfed, skated, played guitar, did karate, and could swim like nobody's business. He reminded her of her dad - a multi talented guy. Her dad might have issues, but he was a good guy at heart, and was very talented at just about everything.

Kyle was popular in school, and Emma liked that since she was so quiet. Dating Kyle distracted Emma from her everyday life. She was tired of the responsibilities that she had at home...taking care of the house chores, cooking, and watching the kids. She was overwhelmed, and that entailed watching her brother and sister, as well as handling household chores and cooking. Her brother was a teenager now too, and was entering into a sudden "cool" phase.

David had become a tall handsome boy...smart and popular in his grade. Emma just retreated into a world with Kyle. She was not allowed to go out and socialize, she didn't have nice things to wear, and was not allowed to wear makeup. She had not learned how to do her hair either, so she just became immune to others' reactions and comments. Nothing affected her after all she'd been through. She built another layer of protection that outwardly appeared to be confidence, but in reality it was an emotional disconnect from everything and everyone in her life. This cute boy at school who called her "Pretty Eyes" had become a welcomed distraction.

"Michelle, I really want to date him. He's a good guy...his name is Kyle, and he's a senior but we are the same age."

Emma and Kyle officially started dating, but that only meant that they were allowed to see each other at school...never after. The good news was that he lived nearby, so he would stop by sometimes during the week after school, but only when her dad was home. With him would be a beautiful rose that he had cut from someone's garden on his way to see her. She knew it probably was wrong, but she thought it was romantic.

"Isn't it beautiful, Dad?" Al noticed a bit of light come back into her eyes since she'd met Kyle, but he wasn't too thrilled that his daughter was dating.

"Dad, if he comes to church with us sometimes, can he then visit me at home?" Emma was hopeful. She knew that kids were dating at a very young age so she wondered why life was so difficult for her. She was 18, and was asking if she could date.

"Okay, Emma that seems fair, but not today, okay?" Emma smiled inside. When they got home from church, she noticed a rose on the gate. "He came by!" she exclaimed. Michelle smiled at her since she understood how much this gesture meant to Emma.

Emma could not wait for Monday to see her super-cute surfer boyfriend. Although Emma was very shy, Kyle was such a good spirited, down-to-earth boy that she felt comfortable with him, and slowly let herself be known like she never had before.

They became best friends and were head-over-heels in love.

A few weeks later Emma got some good news. "Emma, guess what?" David came running over. "Sarah is coming to visit!" Emma's eyes opened wide. "What?!" She had not seen her sister since she herself was 10 years old which made Sarah 4 ½ at the time. She didn't know her that well, so she was excited to be able to spend some time with her, and get to know the now 13 year-old.

They arrived at the airport anxious to greet another sister...she missed having sisters. Emma turned around when she felt a tug on her shirt...it was Sarah. Emma hugged her and kissed her hello. The first thing that Emma noticed was that she looked like her, but with tan skin and brown eyes.

She was cute as could be...sassy and confident...nothing like Emma was at that age. Emma loved her family, but she did notice the difference between her sisters and herself. They were raised with their mother in New York, while Emma and David were raised with their father in Puerto Rico - they were different. They spoke different languages, and had different cultures. Emma felt a bit of envy because she felt that her sisters had personal freedom and she did not.

"Dad, why can't I go to the prom with Kyle? It's his senior prom." Michelle was shaking her head no to Al. Neither one would allow her to go. She walked out of the room upset. She wished that she had the courage to rebel and just go. Emma thought about it, but she couldn't do it...she was always so obedient. She wondered if it would ever be worth it. Kyle would have to go by himself - very disappointed - and Emma cried that night, hoping that he would not be mad at her. "Dad," Sarah said. "She is 18 for God's sake...you can't say no to her. She can basically do whatever she wants."

Emma was appreciative of her sister's fighting spirit, but to no avail - prom came and went. She only hoped that she could attend her own prom the following year. Kyle was upset but patient, and understood why she could not join him. He came over the next day and spent a few hours with her. On Sunday he attended church with her. They had a very innocent and lovely relationship...they were happy. Emma met his mother and she knew his brother from school. Kyle met her family as well. But then Sarah had a great idea.

"Emma, you have to come with me, how fun would that be? Katie is paying for your ticket, and you can see mom again. You haven't seen her in eight years!" Emma was nervous but excited. Things were falling apart at home between Emma and her dad. "Maybe it is best to be away when this all goes down," Emma thought. She needed to talk to her dad because she truly loved him, and didn't want him to lose yet another family.

"Dad, why are you never home? It feels like the old days. Why would you risk losing another family? Why can't you keep it together, Dad?!" He didn't have an answer for her. She knew that he was dealing with his own demons so she decided that it was time to take a break and go see her mother.

"Okay, Sarah I'll come with you...at least for a little while." Sarah screamed with joy! Emma wasn't sure what to do with her life, but she decided to leave because it was the only option she felt that she had. She was still in high school, so where would she go, what could she do?

"Michelle, I am going with Sarah. I can't be here with all that is happening." Michelle knew it was the right decision for Emma right now.

Emma and Sarah would be leaving in a few weeks. She felt nervous and unsure, but it was time. She wanted to see her mother, but she had a new boyfriend that she didn't want to leave behind, and a brother and sister who needed her.

It was time to talk with Kyle. "Why are you leaving, Emma?" Kyle looked sad. "I'm not going for good, but I have not seen my mother in eight years. Also, Kyle, things are not good at home, and I can't be here for that." Kyle understood...he just didn't want her to leave.

"I'll come to see you when I visit my dad in New Jersey." Kyle hugged her and said, "I love you, Emma." Emma's eyes popped open. They had not said that to each other yet. She smiled between tears. "I love you too, Kyle. Please write to me, okay?" For now, they would have to wait to see each other again, and to see how their relationship would evolve.

WHERE IS HOME?

Emma and Sarah were on the airplane ready to take off. Sarah was so excited she kept telling people about her sister from Puerto Rico. "Wow, you have been away from home for eight years? You are going to walk into a party at home," some random lady said. Emma thought about how nice that would be. They arrived at the airport, and Katie was there with a friend to pick them up. Emma ran into Katie's arms.

"I missed you Emma!" Emma smiled and they all got in the car to leave. "How do you feel about seeing Mom?" Emma thought for a minute... she was mostly happy to see Katie. "I'm nervous but happy. I hope she remembers me." Emma's comment hurt Katie because it reminded her of their separation.

"Emma, it might not have been easy for me to live here, and maybe Mom and I didn't get along the best, but of course she remembers you and loves you." Emma knew Katie had moved out a while ago. She knew everything would be different during her stay. When they arrived at their mother's apartment, the same apartment Emma left from back in 1978, they rang the doorbell and waited. Susan opened the door and let everyone in...there was no party.

Susan looked at her 18-year-old daughter...a far cry from the 10-year-old that left New York on that dreadful day. She hugged her quickly, then closed the door, and they walked into the apartment together. The apartment seemed smaller than Emma remembered it, but it was basically exactly the same. Susan had a friend over, and Emma looked around for some sort of 'welcome party' or cake or something. She stared at her mother looking for something familiar, and although she was still beautiful, she was not the same. She felt disappointed that she did not receive the long-lost lingering hug from her mother that she needed. Emma attributed that to leaving NY as a 10-year-old child and returning eight years later as a young adult just like her mother saw her now...not the same kid.

As months passed, Emma felt out of place. She didn't feel like it was her home anymore, and although she knew this new high school was better for her than where she had been, she hated it. It was a completely different culture and she was no longer a New Yorker. She wasn't doing well in school. She couldn't focus and didn't want to be there.

"Emma, you need to do your homework and do better in school." Susan didn't understand or perhaps, accept the different lifestyle that Emma had been living, and Emma was not used to having the freedom to do whatever she wished. She might not have liked the strictness that she grew up with, but she didn't like the unmonitored freedom she now had any better. "Mom, I try - I just want to go home." Emma loved her mother, but the bond they once had was gone.

One night, Emma went out with Sarah at a youth group event nearby, and someone brought wine coolers. Emma had never drunk alcohol in her life so after 1 or 2 wine coolers, she was in bad shape. She and Sarah headed back home. "Mom," Sarah called out. "Here is your innocent daughter from P.R. - she's bombed!" Sarah laughed and Susan wasn't happy. She knew her daughter wasn't used to certain things, but then she laughed when Emma acted silly and started singing loudly. Emma suddenly stopped. "I feel sick!" She ran to the bathroom and threw up. "I don't feel well and the room is spinning." Susan helped her with the pull-out couch. "Come on, lay down, I can't believe you got drunk," Susan told her. Then all of a sudden Emma cried...she cried hard. Susan looked at her.

"What's the matter, Emma?" she asked her. Emma whimpered, "I want Kyle. I want to go home." Susan sat next to her and kissed her forehead as she held her. "It's okay, Baby...Mommy's here." She kept repeating it as if the 10-year-old little girl she left behind needed to hear it. Emma didn't know what she needed, but right now all she wanted was her boyfriend and to go home...wherever that was.

The only thing that kept her sane was Kyle's letters, especially the one with a pretty gold ring he sent taped to a card. She was beaming with happiness and hoped they'd be together forever. It became as clear to Emma as it was to Susan that she needed to go back home, so she decided to go home after Christmas.

"Mom, I just miss home so much and the beach and warm summer." "...and Kyle?" Susan smirked. Emma smiled since she knew he was coming to visit for Christmas and she could not wait. "Yes, especially Kyle. Mom, I'm going to marry him." Susan smiled. She knew her daughter was raised differently, and she could not change how she felt, so she let her go. What else could she do now, but let her go?

"Sarah, that must be Kyle ringing the bell, can you get it?" Sarah ran to get the door. She was excited for her sister even though she was not happy that she would be leaving. When Emma walked to the living room, there was handsome, tan Kyle...a beach boy from Puerto Rico in a coat! It was almost comical. Emma ran to him and they held on for a while. This was the hug she needed all along...someone familiar who loved her. The time she spent with Kyle was wonderful, but different than when they lived in Puerto Rico...they missed it. "Kyle, I really want to go home. I hate it here even though I am worried about what I'm coming home to because I think that Michelle left with Raquel, and has gone to her mother's house." Kyle sympathized. "I know, but the most important thing you need to do is finish school, and then we have to figure out college...one thing at a time." Emma laid her head on Kyle's shoulder. She felt blessed to have someone who understood her and didn't care about her circumstances.

A couple of weeks later it was time for Emma to say goodbye again. Kyle had already left. "You have everything, Emma?" Susan asked her. "I do...let's go." Susan didn't feel up to it. "I'm staying here, Honey. Go with your sisters." Emma was disappointed. "What? You're not coming?" Susan hugged her. I'll see you soon, I hope. I love you, Emma." Katie grabbed Emma's hand, and Sarah followed. Susan closed her apartment door and cried in silence.

CHOICES

Things had changed as Emma suspected. Michelle had left their home with Raquel. Al was alone again, and even though Emma understood the reasons, it was still difficult to see her father in pain, and she worried about her brother.

"Dad, why didn't you fight harder?!" Emma scolded her father for letting Michelle go. "I have lost another sister, Dad." Al was not in the right frame of mind, so even though he felt pain, he buried it within himself and retreated.

Emma knew addiction. She knew it didn't matter what was happening in the addict's life, as it was almost impossible for them to connect to anyone. David and Emma were used to being abandoned at this point. They only had each other, and it made them closer. It was no surprise their dad didn't come home sometimes. Even though they didn't like it, that's what their life was at the moment.

No parents…again, no food…again, and the little Emma made working on Saturday's for just $18.50 for the day at her uncle's pharmacy would be spent either on a quick lunch or on a movie with Kyle. The only good thing Emma had at the moment was Kyle, and she held onto their love. It was a tender, innocent, but strong love.

Kyle was a senior and Emma a junior when they met. They had each other, but mostly Emma had Kyle because no one else was there for her. She had no hope, no goals, no inspiration...only love in her young heart for Kyle. She loved him the best she knew how. "Emma, you have to go college," Kyle's mother said. Emma knew she was right. "I do...I know. I just always thought it was above me...I mean, but can I?"

Kyle's mother knew Emma was in an unstable family situation, but she wanted to help her. "I will help you...don't worry. What was your score on your college boards?" Emma looked worried. "I didn't take it...I moved a lot. This is the 3rd high school I have attended, so I think I missed the deadline." Emma felt frustrated by how clueless she was.

Emma chose to attend a business school that did not require SAT scores. She graduated with an "Associate Degree in Computer Programming," and did very well despite her unorganized, chaotic life at home.

"Dad, why are we moving back with Grandma? Can't we get a place of our own?" Emma knew the answer to that, but she needed to put it out there anyway. "Emma, we have to start over, and the only way we can is if we live with Mom and Dad." She knew her dad was in the middle of a divorce, and was going through his own life drama.

"I don't know what to do. I just can't live with my grandfather after what he did to me? Doesn't anyone realize that?" Emma told Kyle and his mother during lunch one afternoon about what was going on. "Stay here," Kyle's mother said. Emma and Kyle both looked at her surprised. "What?" Emma asked. "You can stay here temporarily and in separate bedrooms of course, if you help with groceries. You shouldn't have to stay with that man! " Emma felt relieved, and thanked her for understanding. Kyle looked happy about the decision. She accepted the offer until she could figure out what to do next, because it was not exactly what she wanted. She wanted to enjoy school, find a good job, and get married, but she needed a helping hand. "Thank you so much, Esther. I really appreciate it!" She felt relieved.

It didn't take long for Emma to realize that she was intruding on her boyfriend's life by living in his house, and it definitely was not what she wanted to do.

"Kyle, where are you going?" she asked him one afternoon. "To play basketball. I'll be back." She wondered why he didn't ask her to go with him. "But we haven't hung out together since I've been here." As he was leaving, he yelled out, "What are you talking about...you live here." He seemed annoyed at her, so she stopped bothering him. "I have to save money and move out somehow, otherwise we won't survive," she said to herself. There was no one she could consult with - she was on her own.

After work one day, Kyle went to pick her up and she sadly gave him the news that her company had gone bankrupt and she'd lost her job. "They let everyone go today, Kyle." He held her close. "It's okay, we can go to the beach." He winked at her. "Yes!" She smiled. "Of course...the beach, but we also need jobs. Hey, why don't we go on job interviews next week? We can look in the paper." Kyle might not have been so quick to need a job since he had parents that cared for him, but Emma didn't...she needed to work. After a couple of weeks of interviewing, Emma got a few offers, but Kyle didn't get any. "It's okay, Kyle, you can try a different place." She saw how upset he was, so she decided not to take the jobs. "I'm tired of this, Emma. I'm not going to find anything good here in Puerto Rico." She tried to console him but he seemed to be somewhat mad at her. She knew if she was able to live at home, wherever that was, she would have taken the job immediately, but having Kyle go through it with her made it a bit difficult. "Should we try New York? Your dad is there, my mom is there, and we can still be together. I mean, I can't continue to live here... it's not appropriate." Kyle knew she was right. "Yeah, let's do it. I can't find anything here."

The next day, Kyle spoke with his mother, and then called his father in New Jersey to tell him that he would be moving there for a bit. Emma called her mother as well. It wasn't easy, because she didn't want to leave her island, but she felt she had no choice.

"Hi Mom." "Oh, hi Emma, how are you?" "I'm okay. Um...I was wondering if, um I can come live with you for a little while? I don't have anywhere to live at the moment nor money to get my own place." Her mother responded, "Yes," immediately.

"Of course...you are my daughter and I am your mother. Come live here. You need to get your life together, and New York is the perfect place to do that." Emma knew she was right. She felt unsettled, but it was time to try their luck in New York. "Emma, maybe this will be good for us. We can move in together as soon as we save enough money. I don't want to be away from you anymore." Emma thought she heard wrong.

"Um, you mean get married..." she answered. "I don't want to be away from you either, but living together was never on my mind." Kyle looked at her. "Yeah, maybe one day, but for now let's get out of our parents' houses." Emma was not happy about it, but Kyle convinced her. If they were going to try New York, they would do it together.

As time went on, they felt forced to move again. Even though it was their decision from the beginning, it weighed on them. Neither New York nor New Jersey felt like home. "Mom I just don't know what to do. I love Puerto Rico!" Susan understood but she also didn't like that Emma felt that way. "Well, you are home now. You were born here, Emma." Emma looked at her mother not wanting to hear what she had to say. "Mom, yes I know, but I left when I was ten years old...it's just not home anymore" Susan was hurt. "Well, you aren't blaming me for that, are you? I thought you were coming back...your father kept you there." Emma sighed.

"Neither one of you did the right thing," Emma said to her mom. That's all Susan had to hear...to go on and on about how her kids were taken from her. Emma understood it must have been difficult for her mother, but she didn't think that Susan knew how difficult it was for Emma never to see her.

At this point all she could do was give New York a try. She knew she would be back on her island one day. Once she opened up and accepted her life in New York, she started to meet people and create her routine. Months later she met Tracey and they became friends pretty quickly. They shared stories and confided with each other. She was happy to have her because the only person she ever saw was Kyle, and things seemed to be changing between them. She reluctantly got an apartment with Kyle. She loved him, but she felt like they had already started on the wrong foot by not marrying...it meant something to her. "Emma, don't worry...it's fine. Look, I don't want to get married right now, but we love each other and that should be enough. We don't need a piece of paper to tell us we are together." "Kyle, I was not brought up that way. I need to be married and why wouldn't you want to marry? You wrote in all of your letters that you wanted to." Kyle got mad and just promised they would be some day. Emma felt differently about Kyle. She felt that it was a reaction to how he started acting, but she went with it, just like she did everything else.

THE UNEXPECTED

"Kyle, don't yell at me!" she yelled back at Kyle. "There is no reason for you to be this mad." He continued to drive. "I'm sorry, but why were you so late?" She didn't answer. She was getting really tired of this life and of Kyle's yelling all the time. "Kyle," she cried. "What are we doing? I feel like I am more ambitious than you are, why don't you care about where we live, and how we live?" Arguments like this continued almost on a daily basis. They both had jobs and were figuring it out, but living the way they were, in a small apartment didn't look like progress to her.

Emma spent one day with her friend, Tracey...she needed girl time. "Emma, please tell me you don't have the flu. I can't be sick right now." She started to spray Lysol in the room. "No Tracey, it's not the flu. My stomach has just been bothering me lately." She held her stomach as if she were about to hurl. Tracey turned around slowly to face Emma. She put her hand up and shouted, "Wait!" Emma looked at her weirdly.

"What?!?" She started to get up from the couch. "Ugh...I need ginger ale." As she was walking away, she sensed Tracey staring at her. She turned around slowly towards Tracey as she understood what Tracey was thinking. Tracey's arms were crossed and her eyebrows raised. "Yes, Tracey what is it? Oh, come on. You don't think..." Emma stopped as Tracey nodded yes.

"Uh huh," she replied. "Oh God, I think I'm going to faint." Tracey ran over to her friend to assist.

"Okay, okay, let's not panic! Look, we don't know yet, so why don't we buy a test, and see what's what?" Emma nodded in agreement. I'm sure Kyle will be excited. I mean you guys are young - it's not a bad thing to have a baby now." She felt her friend tense up.

"Tracey, I can't be. I mean I can be, but this is not right. I don't want to bring a child into the world this way." Tracey looked at Emma intensely. "What way, Emma?" She knew something was up...she knew her well. She held Emma's hand.

"Emma, Honey...talk to me." Tracey saw the tears start. "Oh okay, okay, Honey. Everything is fine." Emma pulled away.

"No...no it won't. I'm a terrible person, Tracey. You shouldn't be my friend." Tracey knew it was something serious. "Okay, Emma, but I am your friend so tell me what's wrong." Emma turned to her this time. "I don't know if Kyle is the father of this baby." Tracey turned pale! It was bad, she thought to herself. "Oh, my." Emma put her hands to her face. "See what I mean? Oh God, what am I going to do?" Tracey ran to her. "Now you listen to me, Emma. Yes, this is a…bad thing, but no one is perfect, and you guys have been fighting. Okay look, I don't know how this will all play out because this will truly hurt Kyle, but I will always be your friend. I will be here for you." She hugged her tightly. "Thank you, Tracey." "Listen, you must be feeling horrible, and being pregnant doesn't help. My gosh...does the other guy know? Who is the other guy? You never told me about anyone else?" Emma was embarrassed. "No one special... just an 'incident' I mean...it really was just a moment. I mean...I thought I liked him, he told me he was single, and I was having problems, so we just met. But I found out he is dating someone, and now I'm like this!" She cried some more.

"Emma, look we all make mistakes, and I'm sorry that this happened because you don't deserve it, and the baby doesn't deserve it, but like you tell me...God loves you, right? Isn't that what you say? And He forgives, so hopefully you and Kyle can get through this too. Either way, I will be here for you." Emma loved her friend with all her heart. She knew she was right, but she wasn't ready to tell Kyle since she truly didn't know who the father was. "You can do this, Emma. You are the strongest woman I know.

Let me just run to Walgreens and pick up an over-the-counter pregnancy test, and we will do this together, okay?"

Tracey left, and Emma sat to think for a moment about the innocent child she was carrying. She could not believe she had done such a thing that would cause so much pain. She wondered why she had…

"Okay, Baby, if you exist we will find out in a few minutes. I know you can't hear me yet, but I'll try my best to be a good mom. I am so sorry for all of this." Although she felt nervous, there was no doubt in her mind that she would have the baby. She felt a sense of happiness even though, for some reason, she thought that she didn't deserve it. She felt like for the first time in her life...she was getting something that was just hers.

Tracey returned, and the test came out positive...she was pregnant. The girls just looked at each other, then all of a sudden, they both smiled. "Oh my gosh,Tracey! Why are we smiling?" Tracey shrugged her shoulders. "I don't know Emma. I mean I kind of feel happy. It's a little bitty baby coming." Emma smiled but she felt guilty, then felt sick again remembering the bad thing she had done.

A few months later, Emma became comfortable with the idea of having a baby, but she didn't have the heart to tell Kyle, so she hid it. Other than feeling her guilt, her pregnancy was an easy and healthy one. She loved every minute of it! She was fascinated with the process of the baby growing and kicking inside of her.

"This baby is going to be an athlete or a dancer or something, because she/he doesn't stop moving. It's the coolest thing ever!" Tracey put her hand on Emma's belly and felt the baby move. Her eyes opened wide as she jumped back...Emma laughed. "Okay, yup...that is cool!" She got up. "I'll be late for work...gotta run." She paused... "Emma, you need to talk to Kyle." Emma made a face. "I know, I know…I'm going to." Tracey left and Emma thought about what she said, she thought that she might not be able to do it.

"Kyle, can we talk?" He went over to her and put his ear to her baby bump. She sighed. "What is it? You feeling okay? I can't believe we are having a baby. This is scary but amazing at the same time. Do you think we can do it, Emma?" She put her hand on his cheek and took a deep breath. "Kyle…" She looked into his eyes. "Of course, we can." The words that she was supposed to say wouldn't come out. "It will be scary like you say, but I know we can do it." She decided to let it go, after all, he could be the father.

HER LITTLE MIRACLE

Emma was young and healthy, and as her due date got closer, summer was becoming too hot for her. She couldn't wait for the baby to be born. She visited with her mom and Katie one day to get out of her apartment.

"If I don't have this baby, Katie, I'm going to burst. I can't believe my due date passed already." Katie laughed and told her to see her doctor again just to be on the safe side since the baby was late. "The baby must be very comfortable there. I can't wait to find out what you are having." Emma couldn't wait either. Two of her sisters had girls so far and only one boy. She secretly wanted a girl but everyone believed that she was having a boy, so she just believed it.

A few days later, Emma went to her doctor appointments which were scheduled weekly since the baby was late. "Step into this room, Emma. Let's do another ultrasound to see if the baby is ready." Emma followed the nurse to meet the ultrasound technician. She watched the monitor and asked if she could have a picture of the baby. "It's too late for that - you should have asked in the beginning." The technician was not very friendly, Emma thought. "I didn't know I could...no one ever mentioned it." The technician just stared at the monitor as if she wasn't speaking at all, and then he walked out. Emma sat up confused. When he came back into the examination room, the technician told her she would be staying. She thought she heard him incorrectly.

"I'm sorry, what?" she asked. He answered abruptly, "You have no water. You are staying." What did that mean? Emma thought she couldn't understand his mumbling, and he wasn't being very nice. "Staying where?" she asked nervously. "Here, Miss...in the hospital. You have no water." Emma was confused.

"I have no water?! Wait, what?" The technician shrugged his shoulders in annoyance. He acted like he didn't even want to be at work. It made Emma feel lonely. Emma realized what was happening and opened her eyes wide...she was going to have her baby! She was two weeks late after all, but before she could ask if the baby was okay, the technician pointed to a different room and walked out.

"Um, okay... Baby, well I guess it's your day. I'm not sure what to do now, but…" She called Kyle at work.

"Kyle?" "Hi Emma, what's up? You never call me at work." Emma was quiet for the moment of truth was near. She knew the moment was actually here, but she dismissed it. "I'm at the hospital...it's time." "Time for what? Oh! It's time! Oh my God." Emma interrupted, "Apparently my water broke a little at a time over the course of a few days, so now they are keeping me to have the baby. You need to come, Kyle. I'm by myself." She sounded worried. "Emma, I'm working...I don't think I can leave." Emma interrupted, "Of course, you can, what do you mean? Get over here!" Jeez, she thought...could she catch a break? She should have just told him and been done with it, since things between them had not gotten any better. Kyle promised to come and she hung up the phone. She felt empty, like she wasn't present.

She walked over to the room that the technician had pointed to...it was empty. She sat on the bed, and a few minutes later a nurse came in. The nurse looked at Emma and smiled...it made her feel better.

"Hello, Sweetie?" Emma looked nervous. "Everything is fine. I'm just going to take some blood and your vitals, and we will see where we are." Emma nodded. She was grateful that the nurse was nice.

"So, how are you feeling right now?" Emma tried to smile. "Um... nervous...I don't feel anything yet." "Okay, well enjoy the moment because soon a baby will be born." Emma smiled. "I'm going to be a mom." "Yes you are, Love. Don't you want to call someone?" Emma looked at the nurse. "I called my boyfriend. He will call my family to let them know." The nurse smiled again. "Oh, you're not married?" Emma looked at her rather upset, and the nurse turned away. "No matter, you don't need to be. I'm sorry I asked. I'll be here if they can't make it, okay? Right now, let's get you ready. Hold out your arm for me please." Emma did as she was told.

"Do you ever have problems with your veins, Sweetie?" She felt the needle in her arm but didn't see blood going into the tube. "I can't seem to find a vein." "No, I never have a problem." Emma suddenly felt like she was young, single, alone, and being judged. "Okay, no worries. I'll try again." After several attempts Emma was feeling anxious. "Well maybe someone else can do it?" Emma said to the nurse, but she was persistent, and clearly a student with no supervision. That realization hit Emma like a ton of bricks, and she thought that if she was feeling pain through this, what would it be like to have the baby through a dry birth? She was even more nervous now.

After all the poking in Emma's arm, she was bleeding and the nurse simply gathered some of the dripping blood into the tube. Emma looked around as if she were on an episode of 'PUNKED.'

"I really am getting punished." The nurse turned toward her. "What was that, Honey?" Emma's eyes widened...she didn't realize she had said that out loud. "Oh nothing...I heard the pain of giving birth is to punish women." She lied. The nurse chuckled. She didn't know that Emma was referring not only to expected pain, but also to her incompetent blood withdrawal.

"Well, you know that 'Eve' girl? She screwed us with that apple she ate." Emma laughed at that. "Well actually, as Joyce Meyer put it, we could blame Adam because he was put in charge and should have stopped her!" The nurse looked at Emma with a smile.

"Aha! I knew it wasn't our fault. Okay Honey, we are done here." Emma was relieved even though she noticed that the vile was not filled. She wondered what the doctor would say to the nurse when she saw it. "I sure hope so...now go practice with an orange." Emma looked at the nurse to see if she heard that...at this point she didn't know what she was saying out loud or to herself.

"God, can you hear me? Am I being punished? Grandma once told me that you don't punish people...you help us, but I know I have done something bad. God, I have been good my whole life. How could I have done this? God, please help! I don't know what to do about Kyle and this baby."

So far, she had "no water" as the technician so delicately put it, and now the nurse was collecting droplets of blood from her bleeding arm. She sighed. After everything she had been through in her life, she wasn't shocked for more "stuff" to come her way; although this time, she caused it herself. She was antsy...she'd been in the hospital since 12:00 that afternoon, and now it was 6:00PM. The baby didn't appear to be in a hurry to arrive. Tit was like it knew the mess it was coming into. She was happy when Kyle arrived, but nervous too. She was told that she had to be induced. She wondered if her stress had caused the baby to not want to arrive.

"Why do I have to be induced? Won't he come naturally?" she asked a doctor. "Oh, you're having a boy? Congratulations!" Emma looked at the doctor. "What? No...I don't actually know. Everyone just keeps telling me I am having a boy...I just got used to the idea." The doctor smiled. "It'll be a surprise then! We like surprises around here."

Emma stretched. "Can I walk around? I feel the need to walk and I have been laying here all day." The answer was no, because she was to be induced. Getting up would not help. It was driving her crazy that she was not able to get up from the hospital bed. She'd been there since 12:00 that afternoon and needed to walk around.

"Emma, why couldn't you break water like a normal woman?" she thought. She was hard on herself, but it felt as if her life was made for her to suffer through. So far, no good, and she was getting tired of it. Emma was able to get a hold of her friend, Tracey, but she was out of town. Kyle was as nervous as she was.

"Here... I brought you some ice chips." Emma pushed his hand away. "Ice chips?! What is that for?" "I don't know Emma, they just told me to bring them to you." Emma was bored, tired, hungry, and now in pain. "Am I not supposed to eat? I've been here all day!" Kyle went to find out.

About an hour later, as if things couldn't get any worse, the doctor who appeared to be the only one on the floor that evening, walked in with a group of 5 or 6 young people wearing lab coats. "Emma, we are here to check on you, okay? All of us want to make sure you are dilating since we began inducing your labor, and make sure that everything looks normal, okay?" "All of us? What did that mean?" She hoped she had said that out loud, but no words came out...never when she wanted them to. She was confused as to why there were so many people examining her. Kyle looked uncomfortable with men touching her, but he didn't say anything...they were doctors. Emma winced. "It hurts! What are you doing?" "We just need to see how dilated you are, Emma...we are almost done."

"Okay, it's a little early, but we will come by later and administer the epidural, okay?" She nodded yes, and they all left. She'd heard about epidurals, and knew that if she had one, it wouldn't hurt as much while delivering the baby. In the meantime, with her emotions all over the place, she cried, she felt violated, and Kyle was angry. The group came in a couple more times, and Emma was physically and emotionally drained. "Kyle, I can't do this. I'm so tired." "I'm tired too, Emma...I've been here all day." She looked at him disappointedly, and wished she could just blurt out the truth about the baby, but she couldn't...at least she wasn't alone.

At about 5:00AM, Emma started to feel labor pains. They were strong and coming fast. She still had not slept and was exhausted. Kyle had dozed off in the chair but awoke when he heard Emma moan loudly. "Emma, you okay? Is the baby coming? What should I do?" Emma continued to moan, the pain she felt was excruciating. Kyle managed to flag down an intern who passed by their room, he told her to get a doctor. She looked annoyed, but went to find one.

The doctor came in, checked with all of her 'friends,' and said it was time to deliver the baby. "She's crowning...let's go!" Emma was in so much pain. She had been waiting for the epidural. Kyle jumped up and asked "What about her epidural?" Someone answered "It's too late for that. Let's go everyone!" Emma looked at Kyle...scared!

"Wait..what?!" Emma asked out of breath. "I have been waiting for it!" "I'm the only doctor on staff right now, and there are 8 other women giving birth, so I'm running from one to the other." Of course, Emma thought. . .punishment!

They rushed her to the delivery room, and right away told her to push. She had finally learned that all of the doctors 'frends' were interns who were there to learn. She was annoyed since no one had given her the option to allow them to participate or not. Maybe they should study women who are experienced and have already had children, she thought. While her mind was flooded with doubt, she could not help but to worry about what was about to happen...she was going to be a mother. The look on one of the student's faces interrupted Emma's thoughts. She was holding a scalpel and appeared to be somewhat shocked. Right then the doctor grabbed it from her, and showed his anger. "What was happening?" Emma thought.

Kyle, who was watching the whole delivery chimed in. "What just happened? Why is she bleeding so much? Why did you cut her?" Emma winced in pain. The doctor explained that they needed to cut her a little so the baby could come out comfortably. That did not seem like a little, and the look on that intern's face attested to it! Emma was so scared...a baby, delivery emotions, a lie, and she was so exhausted she didn't think she would make it.

After 15 hours in labor, the baby arrived. The baby's eyes were open which surprised Emma. Emma looked down and saw her precious, innocent baby with full lips and eyes wide open as if to say, "Mom, this isn't going to end well." Emma felt a tug in her heart, she knew she would do right by her baby.

"Is it a boy?" she asked since no one said anything, and that's what she thought she was having. "No," someone answered. "It's a girl." They continued working in a frenzy, and then all but two people had left the delivery room...the doctor and that idiot intern. "A girl!" She thought that she couldn't believe her ears. "A girl," she kept repeating in her head. Oh my gosh,,,I have a little girl! She then cried, and felt that she had been given a gift from God that no one could ever take it from her!

She thanked God for this little baby, and watched as they wiped her off and took her away. She memorized every bit of her in case she might disappear. Emma knew she was being paranoid, but she knew it sometimes happened. I'm watching too many "Lifetime" movies, she thought.

"Where are you taking her?" Kyle asked. "They're taking her to clean her up and then to the nursery...she will be fine. Kyle followed them out. He also wanted to make sure that his baby was safe. The two people left in the delivery room were working on Emma, and she still felt a lot of pain.

"Oh, what are you doing? That really hurts!" she cried out. "How can you even feel anything after having a baby?" She sounded sarcastic. Emma could not believe her ears.

"It really hurts! What are you doing?" This time she did speak up...she didn't understand the pain, but she'd had enough of it. The doctor looked annoyed, and the student stressed out. "It's nothing. We had to cut a little for the baby to arrive, and we are stitching you up." Emma realized then why the intern had that look of shock on her face earlier.

"But it hurts a lot! I can feel everything! Why is it taking so long?!" Emma was in so much physical and emotional pain that she didn't want to feel anymore. "Well, there are about 30 stitches or so...do you want us to numb you a bit?" Emma almost laughed out loud, but was in agony, and had not slept yet so she was too tired to argue. "30 stitches??" What in the world had they done to her? She just nodded yes, and again the doctor seemed annoyed.

Emma looked up to see if she could see God somehow. "Lord, why? I know I am not perfect, but do I deserve this? I can't even have a normal delivery?" She thought of Kyle. She knew that she had hurt Kyle. Was this the payback? Was it because I still haven't told him the truth?

She stayed in the hospital for a couple of days. Only she and Kyle were there, so she was happy to be leaving, even while feeling the pain in her body.

THE TRUTH SHALL SET YOU FREE

When Kyle and Emma got home with their precious princess, Emma's family was waiting for them. Tracey had called them to let them know when they would arrive. Emma felt relieved...she needed them. She was still nervous and protective of her baby girl...a feeling of love she had only felt when baby Raquel was born, but she was happy they were there.

"Emma, she's beautiful. I'm so in love with her, and the name you chose is precious...Lyla," Tracey said to her.

When everyone left, she and Kyle sat staring at their newborn. "Emma, I don't want anyone touching her or holding her, okay?" She didn't disagree. Neither one of them had ever felt that kind of love before, and they were terrified of losing it. That made it worse for Emma, because of the lie that she was holding tight.

"Kyle, I need to lie down. She's sleeping so please watch her for me." She tried to rest, but her body did not let her. It was in excruciating pain, and she didn't know why - she thought it was due to giving birth.

3:00AM came and baby Lyla was hungry, so Emma got up to feed her while barely able to move. "Kyle, I want to breastfeed her, but it's so difficult...I can barely hold her." Kyle dismissed her and went back to sleep, but after a few nights of that, Emma had enough pain.

It was after midnight when Emma's body was speaking loudly. She tried to pray. "God, please have mercy on me! Is there anything else I need to suffer through? I am sorry. Okay...I will tell him the truth soon." She was fidgety and it woke Kyle up.

"Kyle, help - I can't do this!" She was crying hysterically. "What's wrong, Emma?" He looked nervous. "I don't know...I can't stand the pain. Shouldn't this be gone by now? I need to go to the emergency room - I can't wait until morning...please, Kyle." Kyle saw the urgency in her face and heard it in her voice, so now was no time to argue. They got dressed, packed up little Lyla, and drove to the hospital. She cried the whole way.

"Emma, why didn't you tell me sooner?" She didn't answer. In the emergency room, after filling out tons of paper, and about five hours of waiting, they called her in.

"I guess emergency means you have to be shot to be attended." Kyle was furious - he hated that Emma was in so much pain, and having his newborn in a hospital full of sick people. Once in the private room, they ended up waiting another hour for a doctor to come in.

"Hi, I'm Doctor Spencer. What seems to be the problem?" He saw the baby carrier. "Oh, did you just have a baby?" He smiled, but neither Emma or Kyle were entertained...they were exhausted.

"Yes, she just had a baby. Look, she's been waiting for a long time. She doesn't feel well. Please check to see what's wrong." The doctor saw the concern on both of their faces. He checked her temperature and vital signs. "You have a very high fever, Emma. Let me check you out further." Emma put on a robe and the doctor examined her. She noticed the surprised and worried look on his face when he finished.

"What?! What is it, Doctor?" He took off his medical gloves, threw them in the trash can and put his hands on his waist. "You have a severe infection caused by the injury you sustained during your labor. You probably should have had a C-section. This is very bad. I am giving you antibiotics that should work pretty quickly, but you need to stay here overnight for observation." She knew it was something other than regular labor healing. She wanted to stay but the look on Kyle's face told her another story.

"She can't stay doctor. We just had a baby and I don't know what to do with her." Emma looked at him hoping that he would change his mind. The doctor interrupted, "Isn't there someone you can call to watch her?" Kyle was not having it. He looked at Emma, trying to get her to answer. She knew he didn't want anyone watching Lyla. "It's okay, Doctor...I will go home." The doctor looked upset, but she signed herself out. There was nothing he could do. "Please follow the prescription and come back to see me if you don't feel any better." They thanked him and left the hospital.

For three months Emma tortured herself while she was home and Kyle worked. She was no longer happy or didn't know how to be, and didn't believe Kyle should be lied to anymore. She knew just by looking at the baby that she was not his daughter. It was time to tell him the truth - she was sorry that she had waited. Once Emma made her decision to tell the truth, she also made the decision to leave. She figured that once she told Kyle the truth about the baby, he would leave her, so she decided to leave instead, beside the fact that she just couldn't face him.

She had Sarah and Tracey come over to see the baby while Kyle worked.

"Guys, it might be the worst way possible of telling Kyle the truth, but I have decided to leave him, and I'm going to write a letter. He needs to know...it's like I know just by looking at her." She watched their jaws drop! "I don't think he will be able to forgive me. For sure he will dump me, call me all kinds of names, and maybe I deserve it." "Wait," Tracey said. "You mean you are going to write a 'Dear John' letter and leave?" Tears welled up in Emma's eyes. "Wow, that sounds terrible doesn't it?" Emma said. "I just can't tell him in person. I can't bear to see the pain I have caused. Oh God, what have I done?" The girls consoled her, but they knew how bad this was, and it was something Emma had to do on her own.

The next morning, she called her mother to see if she could stay there until she was able to go back to work and get her own place. She told her the story and her mother agreed that she could stay with her. All she had to do now was to write that letter and pack some bags.

"Dear Kyle, first things first. . .I love you. . . ." She continued to write the letter explaining how bad she felt about herself and how sorry she was for this terrible thing she had done, etc. She packed, left the letter on the table and walked out. "Mom, I don't know what to do." Susan was surprised at what Emma had done...she was good.

"Well Emma, there is nothing you can do now, but wait. No, this is not good, but you are my daughter and I support you." Emma realized she was doing what her dad always did...run. Maybe her dad wasn't taught to face his challenges, or how to deal with them - she wasn't either. They waited until they knew Kyle had gotten home from work. Surely, she would get a phone call from him.

The phone rang and Emma stood up quickly...she was so nervous. Susan picked up the phone. "Yes, Kyle, she is here safe...they are both safe." She handed the phone to Emma, but Emma waved her away. "You have to take it! This is your problem." Emma slowly grabbed the receiver. "Hello?" The dreaded moment had come. "Emma, Emma please tell me this is not true. How could you do this?" Emma felt a sense of loss and just wanted to end the call. She didn't want to deal with it or anything anymore. She was tired of life. All she could say was, "I'm sorry, Kyle. I didn't know what to do. I'm sorry I hurt you." She let Kyle vent and cry, and vent some more over the phone until he announced that he was coming to get them. "No, Kyle! I'm staying here. I don't think we should be together anymore...look what I did, Kyle." He hung up and she knew he would show up soon.

"Mom, he's coming over." Susan was annoyed. She had two little kids at home and didn't need this drama in her home. "Mom, I'm sorry - I just need to be here. Maybe he will leave quickly." They both knew that wouldn't happen. About an hour later he showed up; Emma went to the door. She couldn't believe he drove in that condition. "Kyle, why did you drive here?" He walked in and addressed Susan. "Susan, how could she do this to me?" He was clearly upset and getting loud. "Look Kyle, no one is perfect, but listen, I have two kids here and I don't want them to hear this. Please go into the room and talk." Emma grabbed his arm and they went into the room, while Lyla slept in the other room.

"Where is she? I need to see MY baby!" It was clear to Emma that Kyle was not himself and he wasn't about to give up on this baby. "She's in Mom's room." He got up and went into the room. Emma followed in case he got the idea to take her, but all he did was pick her up and cry over her. "Emma, how could you do this?" Emma, nearly collapsed. She could not believe what she had caused, and realized what a mistake it was to not tell him sooner. He looked at her differently. She could see it, but she expected it.

"You guys are coming with me...HOME...now!" Emma didn't want to - she wanted him to leave. "How could this get better from this moment?" she wondered. He walked into the living room with the baby and again complained to Susan.

"Kyle, I'm so sorry - I know this can't be easy, but she had to tell you the truth." He gave her an angry look.

"Now, you tell me?!" he yelled out. "You tell me after we've lived together through your pregnancy, loving you and the baby...hoping... dreaming about my baby? This is not right!" There was no argument there, and as much as Emma knew it probably wasn't a good idea to leave with him, she did - but not before looking at her mom hoping she would intervene and stop her. She didn't and they left. Emma felt hopeless.

On the ride home, it became clear to Emma that it was a huge mistake to leave with him. She sat in the backseat with the baby in the car seat, and he almost immediately threw a punch at her. Emma was shocked! He had a temper but was never physically violent. "Kyle, what are you doing? Let me out then!" He threw another punch and it hurt her...she cried. "Kyle, you have every right to feel this way, but you can't just hit me. Why am I going back with you then?" He started screaming in the car.

"Kyle, stop! The baby is in the car seat. Stop screaming!" He didn't listen and the screaming didn't stop until they reached their apartment. She wanted to leave as soon as they got there.

He became violent with her and even though she understood the anger, she didn't think it was right to take it out on her that way. "My dad never wants to see you again!" he yelled out. "I am embarrassed. Do you know when I got home, Dad was waiting for me and told me my lights were out. We thought you were at the store or something. He came up with me and saw the letter before I did. Do you know how that made me look?!" They put the baby in the room, and the arguing continued until morning. He wouldn't stop asking who the father was or why Emma did it. "Kyle, it was some guy. You don't know him and that's that. As far as why it happened, I don't have an answer." Despite her understanding the pain he was in, she too was in pain and wanted to end her life. Lyla was the only thing that held her back.

"Kyle, Lyla is three months old now, and I have to get back to work." He turned to her and kicked her. "You are never going back to work. You are staying here and taking care of our baby." She was mad at herself for being scared. Kyle was different and she feared for her life. A man in that kind of pain is capable of anything, but maybe she deserved it she thought.

Emma stayed home with Lyla for her first two years of life. She was happy too even though she missed working. Lyla was a beautiful child, inside and out, and the light of her life. She taught her as much as she could to be good and kind while she was home, despite Kyle yelling, screaming, and hitting her in front of the baby. Lyla quickly learned to be quiet when he was around. "Kyle, don't you see how she reacts around you? She is terrified of you! Look at her put her little fingers in her ears, Kyle." Emma tried to leave him several times since nothing was getting any better. "Is this how it is going to be? You are punishing me while we raise her?"

"Emma, I still love you and I hate you too. I don't' know how to feel about you, but I love Lyla too much, and I don't care if she's not mine." She looked at him. "Kyle, you are not loving her by scaring her. She shouldn't be raised like this. Kyle, please I love you too, but let me go." It was almost as if Emma needed his permission, but she didn't know why.

After two years living in fear, depression, and sadness for her baby, Emma decided it was time to leave. She knew it was not healthy for Kyle either. Emma was stronger now because she knew that living with Kyle was not good for her...especially not for Lyla. Kyle knew it too, but he couldn't let go, so she had to do it. She called her sister, Sarah and asked her if she could help her to leave. It was the only way Emma thought, but this time she would not come back. Sarah and Emma packed up as much as they could and left. Kyle called her and all he did this time was cry. He didn't show up, but he did ask Emma to come to visit with the baby, and she did. She knew she was strong enough now to walk away and raise a child on her own.

"Kyle, I'm coming over today. Will you be home?" Despite Emma being afraid of Kyle at one point, she no longer feared him. She worried that Lyla would not want to be around him, but she kept asking about him, so she decided to take her along to pick up some things. When she showed up one day, Kyle was already crying, and he got down on one knee. Emma was confused. "Emma, please stay. I'm sorry I didn't marry you. I know it was my fault too." But she couldn't stay...it was over and they both knew it.

THE MYSTERY MAN

About a year later, it was determined that Kyle was not Lyla's father and he went back to Puerto Rico. "Emma, I am so sad about this. I still love you, and I will always love Lyla." Emma knew it was true. "I'm sorry, Kyle. I know it is good for you to go back home." She left it at that and felt sadness in her heart. "Tracey, how could a relationship so beautiful turn into crap like that?" Tracey put her hand on Emma's, almost as if to reassure her that everything would be okay.

"On the bright side, Emma, it's been a year - when will you date again?" She changed the subject when she saw the look on Emma's face. "Okay, look we need someone to help out at the bookstore. It's your favorite place to visit and you really should leave that crappy job you have. Work there for a bit until you find something more solid. We can work with your schedule, since you have Lyla to take care of." Emma agreed. "Great...see you Monday."

Emma enjoyed working at the bookstore while her mom took care of Lyla, especially alongside her best friend Tracey. They were both very good with their customers. They had their regular customers and sometimes new ones, and they were always ready to cheer them up when they came in. They had fun making up stories about them. There was this one woman that came in every morning carrying a bouquet of fresh flowers. She would walk up and down the aisles looking for random books and would buy them. Her made-up story they decided was that the woman had a secret admirer who would leave flowers for her in a different spot every day and she would have to find them. She always looked happy and it made them happy.

Another story was about a kind, older gentleman who came in, and he could always be found by the gardening section. They decided he was thinking about his long-lost wife who would garden in their home, and being in that section brought her back. But every time he came in, it made them sad because somehow that story seemed too real. "Hey Tracey, maybe we should find a way to introduce him and that nice lady with the flowers one day." Tracey laughed.

After about six months, Emma changed her shift at the bookstore to weekends only, in order to focus more on her second job at a law firm. She was doing really well there and needed the better pay and health insurance benefits for the baby and her.

"You look good, Emma." Tracey said to her friend during their lunch break. "Thank you, Tracey." "I miss spending more time with you at the store, but the law firm suits you." "Yeah, I miss working with you too, Manager." She shoved Tracey teasingly.

"Yup, that's right. It's 'Miss Manager' to you...thank you very much."

Just then, Emma's eyes fixated on a mystery man. It was a new face at the bookstore. He was a very handsome, distinguished man. He started to come in every day around noon. Emma found him to be handsome and interesting, so she pretended that he was her secret admirer and that they would live happily ever after. Whenever he saw her, he smiled as if he knew her thoughts and she blushed. She thought about him often. She didn't know what it was about him that drew her to him, but she would get nervous every time she saw him.

He came to the store on and off for about a year before he spoke a word to her. One rainy day, it was slow at the store, but Emma hoped that at least her mystery man would show up. Just when they were an hour away from closing and she was losing hope, she heard the bell ring on the door. She glanced over and there he was...her mystery man. He was wearing a raincoat and had a large black umbrella. He looked quite distinguished.

He closed his umbrella and set it in the umbrella stand, hung up his coat, and walked in.

He walked towards Emma and smiled. She hoped he wouldn't notice the redness in her face from blushing when she noticed his dimples and his tall elegant form. "Tall, dark and handsome" came to her mind.

"Hello," he said. She looked at him and she was a little shaky as she heard his deep-toned voice. Tracey was standing next to her and shoved her arm to try and snap Emma out of her "frozen" state. Emma quickly replied, "Hi." "Um...can I help you, Sir?" she asked.

"Yes...please. I would like to sit down for a cup of coffee if that's okay. I just want to get out of the rain before I head home." He smiled again. She melted as she tried to sound professional.

"Yes, of course! Have a seat and I'll get you your coffee," she said nervously. She brought his coffee to him with hands shaking. "Here you go, Sir," she said.

"Mitch," he said. She looked at him with a question in her eyes. He said, "My name...it's Mitchell, but everybody calls me Mitch. Thank you for the coffee." "Oh!" she giggled. "I'm Emma. It's nice to meet you, Mitch." She held out her hand and he took it in his. She felt warmth and electricity soar through her whole body! Whether he noticed that or not she was unaware, but she needed to get away from the table quickly. His dimples alone melted her...never mind her hand in his. So, she removed her hand from his and walked away in a hurry.

"Emma!" he called out, and she turned toward him. "Would it be possible for you to join me?" Emma stood there for what seemed like an eternity. She looked at him confused. He repeated, "I think you're probably done for the day. Would you like to join me for coffee?" His hand was directed towards the empty seat in front of him. When she finally was able to catch her breath, she answered,"Sorry, I can't tonight, but thank you." She really wanted to join him, but she needed to get home to her daughter. She turned away and found Tracey glaring at her. She could almost read her mind... "Are you crazy? Turn around and say 'yes' to that tall, handsome drink of water." Emma made a face at her, and turned back towards Mitch, but before she could say anything he spoke. "Husband?" he asked her, hoping he would hear that she was single.

"Oh, no... I'm single. It's my daughter...I have to get home to her." She looked at Tracey again. "She must be beautiful!" Emma smiled at the compliment. "Thank you." Mitch smiled at her as if to show off his dimples on purpose, and she blushed. "You sure I can't treat you to one cup?" Those dimples she thought... "Ok, sure, I guess. Thank you."

"Please..." He smiled again and pulled out a chair.

Emma was a bit nervous, but he was like a magnet and she couldn't resist, she sat down and heard Tracey yell out, "Yes!" They both turned to look at her friend, Tracey who was obviously happy that she accepted his invitation. "I said that out loud, didn't I?" Emma nodded with embarrassment.

"Okay then...well I'll be over there if you need me." Mitch laughed... Emma was mortified.

"So, Emma..." He smiled at her. "I've been coming in here for a long time and I've always wondered what your name was. I even made up a few names for you." he said. Emma blushed.

"You did?" she said rather surprised. "Well, let's hear them." He smiled and all she could do was stare at his dimples. "Well, at first I thought it was Michelle, then I thought Lyla." Her eyes widened at that. "Lyla? That's my daughter's name." He smiled with surprise. "Well, what do you know. Well..." said Mitch. "I decided not to wait, and asked around, so I knew your name…Emma. It suits you." She blushed. "You're a very beautiful woman, Emma." "Thank you," she replied.

"So, you have a daughter. How old is she?" he asked. "Lyla is 3. She's the best thing that ever happened to me." He smiled and they talked for a bit more before they closed the store. They walked out together. It was then that Emma noticed that he was tall...she liked that. He was also a lot older than she was, but it didn't seem to matter. The chemistry was definitely there. He asked her out to dinner Friday the next week and she accepted.

Emma thought about Mitch every moment of the day that week. She couldn't focus much on work...she was so excited. Tracey had offered to watch Lyla so Emma felt comfortable having a night out...it had been awhile. Friday finally arrived. Tracey came to Emma's apartment early to help her prepare and to babysit.

"So, tonight is the big night, huh? How do you feel?" Tracey asked. She already knew the answer when she saw about 10 outfits on Emma's bed and her hair in a mess. She turned to look at little Lyla who was watching the dress show and made a face. Lyla put her hands up as if to say that her mom needed help, so Tracey winked at little Lyla and decided it was time to intervene.

"Ok, enough!" Tracey put her hands up to stop Emma from panicking. "Put the black one on...the one with the spaghetti straps." Emma stared at her quite confused.

"Emma, if you try on one more dress, I'm changing my mind and I'm going home." Emma knew she was joking, but she listened to her, and put on the black dress. "It's not too much?" she asked Tracey. "Too much for what...a hot date? Emma, I guess you have not yet realized that you are going on a hot date." She grinned and Emma laughed at that. She kept the dress on and fixed her hair.

"So how do I look?" Emma asked. "You look like you're asking for it." Tracey said jokingly. Emma turned red. "What?! But you said…" Tracey stood up. "I'm kidding...geez! You look amazing, now get going." Emma relaxed and looked at little Lyla who said in her little voice, "You look 'butiful,' Mama," as a 3-year-old would say. Emma smiled and kissed Lyla on the cheek. "Just like you, my little angel girl." Lyla giggled. Emma looked at Tracey...hopeful and appreciative.

"Thank you so much for watching her. Remember, no candy or soda. She'll keep me up all night." Tracey crossed her fingers and put her hand behind her back as she winked at Lyla. She pushed Emma out the door before she had a chance to change her mind. "Okay, little angel face...who's ready for candy and soda?" Lyla opened her eyes wide... "Meeeee!" Lyla ran after Tracey towards the kitchen.

Dinner went well. Emma felt comfortable and they talked with ease. Mitch talked about his career, his family, and his childhood, while Emma listened bright-eyed. She loved listening to him. His deliciously deep voice reached the depths of her soul. This was a new feeling for her. She never thought about having a new boyfriend after her last break up, and she now had a little girl to take care of, so she didn't date much. She was hopeful about Mitchell even though they'd just met. She felt close to him already, and he was so handsome she couldn't stand it. He was everything she never knew she wanted, and he made her feel like a woman, and more importantly, like she mattered. Mitch chose an elegant restaurant and she got a kick out of all the attention she was getting from the owner and staff. When dinner ended, Emma felt anxious. She didn't want the evening to end...it was magical! When they left the restaurant, Mitchell took Emma's hand into his as they walked a couple of blocks to his car, and she was perfectly okay with it. He drove her home and they sat in the car for a bit. She was very shy, so she had not said very much at dinner and that was fine because he had a lot to say.

He held her hand and told her that she was beautiful and that he wanted to see her again. She nodded yes. No words were coming out of her mouth. She was unsure as to what he saw in her...it was a surreal moment.

"Emma, I had a great time. Thank you for joining me tonight." Emma couldn't get past the way he said her name and it melted her heart. He leaned over to kiss her and she accepted. The kiss was like fire and they both felt it. She thought she would faint and her hands felt numb. They both pulled away at almost the same time and said their goodbyes. Mitch watched her as she walked to her door. She waved and off he went.

Emma sighed as she opened the door to her apartment, but she didn't have a second to herself before Tracey pounced on her like a cat. Emma was startled.

"How did it go? I've been waiting up. Tell me...did he kiss you? Did you kiss him back? What happened? Tell me everything!" Emma bit her bottom lip and Tracey screamed. "You kissed! You did, you did...I knew it!" Emma was beat red and sat down on her couch with her coat still on. She finally gave in.

"Tracey it was everything I'd hoped for and more." Tracey jumped up on the couch like she had just won something. "Oh my gosh,...spill!" Emma laughed and they both sat down as Emma told her about her magical evening with the mystery man.

THERE WERE SIGNS

Emma fell in love. She hoped to be engaged soon and waited for the special moment that Mitch would propose to her. Kyle hadn't proposed until the day they broke up...it was too late for him, but she had high hopes that Mitch would do so soon.

"Really Mitch, we are going on vacation together?" Emma all but jumped out of her seat from excitement when Mitch told her that they were going on vacation and she couldn't wait. It was their first vacation together as a couple.

"Yes! Are you excited? Other couples will be there too, so it will be nice for them to meet you." Emma couldn't believe how lucky she was to be with someone like Mitch...so educated and important she thought.

"Thank you, Mitch! I am so excited!" Mitch smiled. "You're welcome. Now let's pick out some new things for you to wear...I have some catalogs here." Emma looked at Mitch in surprise. She was humble and didn't expect him to buy her anything.

"Oh Mitch, you don't have to do that. I'm sure I can find some things to pack." But Mitch didn't take no for an answer. He insisted, and started to look through the catalogs...folding pages of what he liked for her. Emma knew he had good taste, so she didn't mind him picking out the outfits... she was having fun. She didn't know that guys did that so she embraced it.

She saw something she liked… "Oh, look at this one...I like the pants and the top is cute." Mitch glanced at the picture. "It is nice, but Emma, I don't think it would suit you. It's more for skinny girls." Emma was confused about what he said, since she was barely a size 3. She quickly dismissed it and chose to enjoy the shopping. She trusted his opinion. After all, who was she anyway? He was worldly, intelligent,and the best dresser in town.

In the next few weeks vacation was all she could think about. She told her friend, Tracey about the trip while they were brunching at their favorite place in the city...Cipriani's.

"Can you believe it? I cannot wait for the beach!" Tracey was sipping her Mimosa when she let out a scream. Emma was startled and looked at her friend.

"What? Are you choking?!" Tracey laughed. "No, silly! Emma, don't freak out okay, but I just thought of something." Emma rolled her eyes.

"No Tracey, you can't come with us." Tracey did a double take and said, "Wait, what? No, Emma I mean that would be nice (and weird), but no, Emma listen to me..."

"What, then?" she asked, confused. Tracey had a weird grin on her face and pointed to her ring finger. Emma's eyes widened and she put her hands over her mouth.

"What?! Noooo...Tracey, stop!" She felt nervous. Tracey kept grinning and pointing to her finger. "Tracey! No, we are just having a little vacation." She knew there was a possibility of a proposal, but she just didn't want to get her hopes up.

"Come on, don't tell me you haven't thought about it." Tracey pushed, but Emma had thought about it only for a nanosecond.

"Okay, well I will say it...Emma, I think he's going to propose. Come on! Okay, here me out...he planned a vacation to the Caribbean, you had an online shopping spree, and didn't he say he was going to introduce you to people?"

"Well, yeah. It doesn't mean what you think it means. It could be...I mean we have talked about it, and Mitch did say he wanted me to be his wife and that he wanted children." She turned to Tracey. "Oh my gosh, do you think so?" She looked at Tracey for reassurance as she watched her mouth the word "pro-po-sal." Emma laughed and gave her a playful shove.

After the conversation she had with Tracey, she couldn't get the thought of marrying Mitch out of her mind. She was nervous but also extremely excited. She didn't know for sure, but the possibility was enough. They arrived at their destination and quickly met up with Mitch's friends and he introduced her to everyone. She noticed she was a lot younger than most, and some looked her up and down as if she didn't belong there. Emma didn't really care... she knew she was a good person and she didn't expect people to understand their relationship.

They were back in the room when Mitch mentioned some of the comments his friends had made. "Well, Ken loves you." He smiled. "Ken's wife...not so much, but who cares. Did you see the shape she was in?" Emma looked at him not at all surprised since she'd noticed the look on Helen's face when she saw them together, but she didn't like what he said about her. "Well, I don't care what people say about me. There is no reason for them not to like me." Mitch looked at her.

"Well it's not like this is your crowd. You probably can't hold a conversation with any of them, but stick with me because we look good together." She gave him a look of surprise. Sometimes he said things that made her uncomfortable. She thought maybe he just wasn't good at describing people. Maybe he was right...she didn't understand what they were talking about.

He continued, "Helen thinks I am dating down." She turned to look at him. "Excuse me?" she asked this time, annoyed. Then she used what he had said earlier about the shape Helen was in. "Well maybe it's just because I am young and attractive?" Mitch turned to look at her with a grin on his face. "You think you are attractive?" he asked as he pulled her towards him. She smiled...she needed him to be on her side.

"Oh, I know I'm attractive or you would never have brought me here." He laughed out loud and they kissed. After a few days of amazing beach bliss, they laid on the beach away from the group for some alone time. She was happy he suggested it since she was tired of being stared at and judged by the group of people who thought they were better than her. She was also tired of being paraded around by Mitch.

She noticed that he was showing off with her, and at first it didn't bother her, but she also really just wanted to spend time with her boyfriend in a loving relationship. As she lay on her comfy hotel beach chair, she remembered what her friend, Tracey had said about a possible proposal and realized it definitely was not happening this time around. Mitch interrupted her thoughts.

"Hey, Babe...can you give me the room key? I need to make a work call." Emma reached for the key in her bag, but couldn't find it. Mitch wiped the sand from his arms and put on his shirt when he noticed Emma rummaging through her bag. "Emma, the key!" She looked at him. "I can't find it. Do you have it?" She knew he didn't, but she took a chance in asking. She noticed the look on his face immediately turned to anger, but it was even more than that and it scared her. "If I had it, I wouldn't be asking you. Where the F is the key, Emma?" Mitch went on a rant grabbed his things and stormed off as Emma stared at him in disbelief of his reaction towards her.

"Come on!" he yelled. Emma was startled...she'd never really saw him react like this. She got her things and followed Mitch. This did not feel right she thought, and she was mad at herself for losing the key, but she knew that the hotel would help them so she didn't think it was so much of a big deal that he had to act like that.

When they reached the front desk, Mitch was yelling at Emma and she knew they noticed his abusive behavior towards her. The hotel manager appeared with a security guard. "Can I help you, sir?" asked the hotel manager. Mitch turned around to face him and the look on his face was intimidating.

"Yes, my girlfriend lost the key to our room. I don't know what the heck she was thinking, but she lost it and I need to get in there." He pointed to Emma who sat down and was crying at this point. "Sir, calm down," they said to Mitch. "Calm down? Get me a key now!" He looked at Emma angrily.

"Get up, Emma. I'm not doing this alone," he yelled out, and some hotel people were staring. "Sir, please..." They pointed to a seat, but Mitch ignored them. "Just wait here and we will get you a new key." Mitch showed them his ID and they gave him a new key. Mitch stormed off. On their way to the room, Mitch continued his rant and he didn't stop until they arrived at a restaurant for dinner with their friends. Emma was beside herself, emotionally disturbed, and confused with his uncalled-for, dramatic and shocking outburst.

She remembered what Tracey had said about a proposal and Emma quickly realized a proposal was not the purpose of this trip. She was there simply to accompany him on a business trip.

The next day, Mitch and Emma agreed they would meet up with the group for a beach day, so Mitch was getting ready, and picked out a swim t-shirt and a hat to match. Emma had already changed and when Mitch saw her, he smiled. "Oh, look at you!" Emma was a bit uneasy from the day before so she turned away from him. "What's wrong?" Mitch asked her. In her mind she was thinking how he could not know, and before she knew it tears ran down her face, so she turned away from him. "Emma?" He turned to her and saw the tears.

"Emma, what happened?" She just came out with it. "The way you acted yesterday Mitch...I've never seen you like that and it made me nervous. You were so angry!" Mitch seemed surprised at what she said.

"What do you mean...when you lost the key? Am I not supposed to get upset about something like that?" She was annoyed by the fact that Mitch didn't seem to think that the way he reacted was unacceptable. No one ever spoke to her like that. He looked at her and knew he wasn't going to win this battle.

"Look...I'm sorry if I yelled. Come on, let's have a good beach day...you look amazing in that bikini!" He grabbed her and held her close as if to tell her, what happened was not a big deal. Emma welcomed it, she didn't want to argue. If she didn't drop the argument then Mitch would escalate it to a whole other level, and she didn't have the stomach for it. It was much easier to let it go. He told her again he was sorry and that he loved her and she believed him. They continued their day and Emma chose to have fun and enjoy the rest of their vacation.

When the last day came his attitude changed. He always got upset when things ended, like a trip. She could see it coming a mile away and tried to stay clear of him, trying not to trigger him. She held her breath on the way to the airport because that's when he also lost it. Leaving their vacation spot was a trigger and it didn't matter how pleasing she was, he would lose his temper on her. She hated it. At times like this, Emma smiled, but felt her body react, as if it were being beaten. She hoped they had a movie screen on their seats, so he would be distracted on the flight.

"Emma, what are you doing?" While onboard, Emma was watching a video on her iPhone. "Watching a video?" Mitch became enraged. "You're what? Watching a video? Why, Emma? Pay me the attention...you don't love me? I'm sitting here and you won't talk to me." He was talking a bit too loud, and a few people looked at him, so he lowered his voice, but his tone remained the same...evil!

"What?!" Emma was confused. What had she done now? "Mitch, you were just watching a movie...what's wrong? You want to talk, just talk and I'll put my phone away." Mitch continued and Emma cried - she couldn't deal with it emotionally. She couldn't get up or leave since she was on a plane. He had her cornered and continued to badger her about absolutely nothing. She didn't understand it, and she felt like she was having a breakdown. She wanted to scream!

When they got their car service at the airport, he talked to the driver as if he had known him his whole life. He was nice and respectful. Emma sneaked a look at Mitch, since he had just spent two hours yelling at her. She couldn't believe how he could switch emotions like that. It was like he had two personalities. She hoped the conversation with the driver would calm him down. When they got home, he turned to her to yell at her again... she couldn't believe it! She broke down and cried on the floor. It was like her body couldn't take it anymore. What was happening to her life? She wondered why she didn't just walk out. She would have to think about that...

THE LITTLE DANCER

Lyla loved to dance. From when she was a baby, she danced to anything, everywhere, and every day. Emma chose a local dance studio and signed her up at 4 ½ years old, and Lyla loved every minute of it...the teachers, the classes, and the new friends that she made. She quickly advanced from regular dance classes to competitive dancing. Emma would never forget Lyla's first recital. She looked so cute in her costume as she danced to "High Hopes." She was so proud of herself, and Emma was surprised at how much she enjoyed being on stage - quite contrary to how Emma was while growing up. Emma and Mitch were proud parents. It didn't take long for them to sign Lyla up for the competition team.

Mitch helped pay for it since it was a bit more money for costumes and fees, but he would never let them forget it. He reminded them every chance he got in case they forgot about his generosity. When Lyla was ready, she had her first solo at a competition recital. She danced to JLO's "Let's Get Loud" - it was a jazz number. She was about 9 years old and it was easy to tell that she was in her element...dance was her joy! When she finished her dance solo, she ran over to her mom and Mitch, who she now called "Daddy."

She wanted to say hello before she moved on to the group dance. She was smiling and hoped that her parents enjoyed her first dance. Emma was beaming with pride, but Mitch, not so much. "Mommy, did you like it?" She ran into her arms and stared at Mitch at the same time. Emma lit up and hugged her little girl tightly.

"Lyla, that was awesome! I loved it! You looked so pretty in your costume." Lyla looked at Mitch, and he smiled at her. "Hi Princess!" She smiled, waiting for her dad to compliment her. "It was good but there are some things you should work on." Emma looked at Mitch in surprise. Lyla's smile quickly faded.

"Did you forget a cartwheel?" he asked Lyla. "Mitch!" Emma exclaimed. His reaction confused and annoyed her. Tears welled up in Lyla's eyes. She looked at her mother as she answered Mitch.

"Daddy, I didn't have a cartwheel in my solo," she gently replied. Emma was furious, and interrupted. "Baby, it was so good! Go get ready for your next dance...see you later, okay?" Lyla kissed them both and ran off, and Emma turned to Mitch.

"What was that, Mitch? It was her first dance by herself and that's all you have to say?" "Yeah, Emma...I pay a lot of money for these things. Why did you say she did great?" Emma waved at Lyla and turned to him with fury in her eyes. She was shocked at his behavior! She couldn't understand it.

"What do you mean, Mitch? It was her first solo...she did great! It is not easy getting up there to be judged. Then she comes to us for approval and you judge her?" Mitch refused to let it go and at dinner, instead of allowing Lyla to join her dance friends after competition to celebrate, he took them to a fancy restaurant to discuss her solo. Lyla cried the whole time and Emma was confused and taken aback at his reaction, and they argued over who was right.

"So here we are at this great restaurant that everyone wishes they could come to, but you guys are all upset." Mitch tried to convince Emma that being tough on Lyla would make her better. Emma disagreed. They finished their dinner and headed home. Emma could see that Lyla was disappointed with her first competition weekend away. Mitch interrupted her thoughts.

"So, Lyla did you have a good time?" he asked, weirdly excited. "Yes," she answered. "You know this weekend cost me a lot of money starting with the costumes, hotel stay, and good restaurants." Emma looked over to him and wondered why he had to bring up what he'd spent. After all, she didn't ask for any of it. She had intended to put her in the competition and figure it out from there, because she really wanted that for her.

"I know Daddy, thank you," Lyla answered. "So that's it, right?" Mitch asked. Emma gave him a quick nod and he dropped them off at their apartment and left.. This was something that Emma was getting tired of. She wondered why he had not asked her to move in yet, and of course, why they were not engaged yet. She loved him, but she was old school, and would never bring it up, although she knew in her mind she should.

She felt like they were already married, so for some reason it was difficult for her to even think about breaking up. But at the same time, being home...just Lyla and her...felt right, so she decided to enjoy the rest of the long weekend alone with her daughter.

So..." she said looking at Lyla. "Should we go to Barnes & Noble?" She felt a little guilty, so she wanted her little girl to enjoy the day. "Yes... it's my favorite store! Can I get a book, Mommy?" Emma nodded. "After how brave you were today on your first solo, heck yes!" Lyla grinned from ear to ear, and off they went.

Mitch called Emma that evening. "Hi,Baby...I miss you." Emma was taken aback. "I miss you too, Mitch," she answered automatically. "Put Lyla on," Mitch said, and Emma hesitated but then called Lyla over. "Lyla honey, Daddy wants to talk to you." Lyla ran in and grabbed the phone. She was always looking for his approval so she would always give in to his demands. "Hi, Daddy!" she said sweetly. "Hi, Princess. I just wanted to say good night. I love you, Baby, and you did really good today. I am proud of you!" Lyla erased what he said earlier and stored this compliment in her heart. She smiled. "Thank you, Daddy...I love you." She hung up and hugged her mom.

"Can you tuck me in, Mom?" Emma was surprised to see how happy Lyla had become. "Oh...um, okay. What did Daddy say?" she asked her. "He said he loved me and he was proud of me." Emma was happy to hear that. She knew he had it in him and was aware this was a new dad who might not know how to father yet, so she let certain things go.

HEARTACHE

"Mitch, can't I come too?" Emma asked. "I'm sorry, Honey...it's just us guys on this trip, but next time I'll take both you and Lyla. I think she'd love it." Emma was happy with that even though she wasn't too comfortable with the idea that he would be away with some guys on vacation...on a sailboat. It didn't seem normal that couples would travel separately on long vacations. She knew he had a life before her, especially since he was 18 years older, and was used to traveling on golfing and sailing trips. Kyle would never have taken such a trip without her. A good sign was that he called her every day and said that the trip was boring, and that he missed her and couldn't wait to come home to her. She was happy to hear that, and waited for his return.

"Hey Emma, I was thinking I would pick you up from the airport before I head home. Is that ok?" Emma was thrilled to hear that. She found a sitter and waited for him to arrive. When he did, and she got in the car, he told her he missed her and held her hand during the entire ride. She was happy to see him and was happy to have an opportunity to spend some time at the house.

When they got there, he went to go settle in, and unpack while she headed to the master bathroom. She looked in the mirror to make sure her makeup was perfect and a glimpse of silk caught her eye. When she turned to see what it was, her heart dropped. There was a woman's robe hanging on the bathroom door...she couldn't believe it! She knew in her heart what it meant, but the denial in her head kept her from speaking. She just wanted them to be okay so she ignored it and figured that when she got up in the morning to take a shower, she would bring up the uncomfortable subject. What she didn't anticipate was that he ended up taking a shower first and when it was her turn, the robe was gone. She felt too awkward to bring it up now since she had not said anything the night before. She felt upset and mad at herself for being afraid of the truth. She wasn't ready to hear it, but still…why didn't she say anything?! What was she afraid of?

On their way to work she observed him to see if he looked any different, but he didn't...he just smiled at her as if nothing was wrong. She knew that he hid the robe and acted as if nothing was wrong with that. "Do you love me still, Mitch?" she asked. He looked like he was in shock. "Of course I do Baby...why do you ask?" She didn't say anything, and looked out the window because she believed in giving the benefit of the doubt to people...also they were not married or even engaged so she thought what right did she have to ask? What she didn't realize then was that she was making excuses for him and accepting his behavior.

Emma never brought up the robe, but something else happened that she just could not ignore. A few weeks later she stumbled upon some pictures in the kitchen drawer of Mitch and another woman, and her heart sank! Not only was he with a woman, but they were on a sailboat. He must have forgotten to put them away because they were left within her reach. The pictures were not hidden, so she didn't think it was an issue to look at them. When he walked in to get some coffee, she asked him about the pictures. He didn't even flinch when he said, "Oh, that's an old friend of mine...they're nothing, Honey. We dated for a long time...there's some history, and I'm still friends with her family." He acted like he would on any other day, kissed her on the lips, and asked her to pass the cream. Emma was stunned...his response was so matter-of-fact.

"Mitch, you're on a boat in this picture, and you went on a boat trip a few weeks ago." He looked at her as if annoyed that she was asking about his life. "Yes, I told you about that trip." She couldn't believe he was not denying it. "Yes, I know Mitch, but you didn't tell me about a woman being on the boat, and she's with you." He sipped his coffee, and then put it down on the kitchen counter. He grabbed her hand and walked into the den and sat down. She couldn't wait to hear what he had to say about this.

"Honey, look... Yes, she was on the boat with me, but I couldn't tell you because I knew you wouldn't understand." That's right...she surely wouldn't she thought.

"Understand what?" she asked. "This woman is a friend of mine. Yes, we dated for a long time and it's hard sometimes to say goodbye to people you care about. I'm with you now, but I had not really broken up 'officially' with her yet." Emma's eyes widened. Was she supposed to understand this?!

"And?" she asked. "And, we already had this trip planned, but I swear we did not get personal. I got through it because I had a commitment... that's all. Emma. I love you so much. Forgive me since I am not invested in her. I didn't think it would affect us. It was nothing but a commitment I had to fulfil." Emma knew it wasn't right. She would never do that to anyone, but she chose to forgive him because he sounded so truthful, as if he truly did not want to harm their relationship.

A few months after the picture incident, Emma and Mitch were preparing to take another vacation to the Caribbean, and she just couldn't wait to get there. She missed being near the ocean. Although again they were not heading to Puerto Rico, she was super excited. The beach was the one place where she felt completely at peace. New York had its advantages but it was a completely different ball game. She didn't care since she thought for sure that this time he would propose. They had been together for a few years now, so it was only logical. She thought about what her friend Tracey said the last time she thought that he might propose...that it was normal at this stage in any relationship, but she didn't want to hear it again, so she didn't tell Tracey that she was going away. In fact, she had not seen her in a while so she just told Tracey that she was busy with work.

One beautiful afternoon they were exploring the island and walking on the beach hand in hand, splashing each other with water and taking pictures. It was perfect, Emma thought.

"Mitch, this is just so beautiful." She smiled. "You're beautiful, Emma," he answered, smiling back at her. The sun was beaming on both of them. Emma didn't mind it, but Mitch was feeling the heat.

"Hey, Honey...can you put some lotion on my back?" She took the lotion out of her bag. "Of course," she answered. She put lotion on Mitch's back and handed the bottle to him. "Can you do me now, Mitch...just to be sure?" As he went to pour lotion on her back, he looked at the bottle and his face changed...it distorted into a very angry face.

Mitch threw the bottle of lotion on the sand, and yelled at her in front of everyone on the beach that she brought the wrong lotion! Then stormed off and left her there!

"What just happened?" she asked herself. She couldn't believe what he had just done. She was waiting for the cast of 'PUNKED' to come out again, to point at the cameras and laugh...only Ashton Kutcher wasn't there, nor were the cameras. She'd seen him have an outburst before, but usually there was something obvious that caused it...like when they got lost on their way to a dinner and he flipped out the whole way there, or when their daughter forgot to take out the garbage, or when his tea was too hot, but this time it was about bringing the "wrong" suntan lotion.

"How could that be?" she wondered. She didn't know what to do or how to feel about what had just happened, so she headed back to their spot on the beach.

She saw him sitting at the chairs talking to one of the beach servers while pouring wine into a glass. She let out a sigh of relief and walked towards him. The server walked away to attend to someone else and Mitch laid back and closed his eyes.

"Mitch, what happened back there? Why were you upset?" He removed his sunglasses and with anger in his eyes (which surprised her after she saw him laughing with the server) said abruptly, "You're kidding, right?!" Emma looked at him confused.

"You don't love me...that's what happened!" Emma shook her head in total confusion and opened her mouth to say something, but no words came out...she was stunned. . .again! He continued, "If you loved me you would have brought the right lotion. I wanted the 15 SPF, not the 45 SPF, Emma. How could you?" Emma had no words, and really just thought he was pulling her leg.

"I'm sorry, Mitch. Didn't know you had a preference, but it's not a big deal." He stood up, and before he stormed off to the bathroom, yelled at her some more.

"Exactly my point, Emma. You don't listen to me. One day I'm going to find someone who really loves me."

"What the heck was happening?" she thought. She felt sad, angry, and defeated. She had no idea why he reacted so angrily...it didn't make sense. Of course, she loved him...what did that have to do with it? She didn't know what to do, and suddenly she wanted to go home. This was far from a proposal. Obviously, she was wrong about that - once again.

It took all day for Mitch to purge the madness that was in his mind. He ignored Emma most of the day, but managed to calm down a bit before dinner. Emma was not up for it, but got ready to go out anyway. Mitch watched her and noticed her sad face.

"Emma, I'm sorry okay? I didn't mean to yell, but Honey, please... you need to listen to what I say." Emma just nodded. She didn't feel like arguing. What she really wanted to do was to go home. It seemed absurd to even her that she didn't just hop on a plane and leave, but she didn't have the courage to do it. At the same time Mitch had become someone that she depended on. If she lost him, how would she ever find anyone else like him? She trusted him, and he loved her so she decided to try harder to make this relationship work so on their way to dinner she grabbed his hand and held it tightly. He gave her his most handsome smile and that was all it took for her to feel reassured that she was important to him.

NEVER A BRIDE

"Emma, can you come in here please?" Mitch called out. He was in the living room with Lyla watching TV when Emma appeared at the doorway. "If it's about this movie, I already saw it." She looked at Lyla who was sitting next to Mitch, smiling like she was keeping a secret.

"Come sit next to me." He put his hand on the couch cushion next to him. Emma walked over and sat down wondering what these two had up their sleeves. He handed Emma a small black box with a small gold clasp that held it closed. She couldn't believe he was about to propose! She looked at Mitch surprised and took the box. They were in the living room at her apartment. It might not have been the most romantic of places, but at least he was about to propose. Emma opened the little black box and it was empty. She looked at Mitch and he handed her a ring...a beautiful sparkly ring. It was exactly what she had wanted. They had talked about it once. She waited for a minute to hear his proposal, but when he didn't say anything, she spoke first…surely, he would say something to her.

"Mitch it's beautiful! Thank you." Mitch proceeded to tell her about the number of carats, the clarity, and how he had it made just for her while Emma held it in her hand...waiting for him to put it on her finger. He didn't, so she put it on herself and realized that it was too big.

"Oh, Mitch it doesn't fit." she told him. "But I got your size...it should fit you. I know you have thick fingers..." Her heart sank at his comment.

"What?! No, but you measured me once, and why would you say it like that? It sounds mean." He didn't respond. He didn't believe her even though the proof was the ring falling off her finger. He continued to talk about the great job he did designing the ring, almost like he cared more about getting the credit for the ring and not what it was supposed to mean. She thought his behavior was strange. She didn't understand him sometimes, but she had waited so long for a ring that she just gave in.

"Well, it's beautiful. I love it. Thank you." She was still waiting for the proposal that never came. She looked at Lyla who was also waiting, but all he did was grab the TV remote control, and watched the football game. So, was this just a gift, she wondered? Once again, she just couldn't get the words out.

Emma and Lyla went into the kitchen. Lyla grabbed Emma's hand and squeezed it. "Mommy, he didn't propose...but it's okay mommy." Emma smiled at her. She knew what she was thinking...it should have been romantic.

"Well, no...but sometimes men are shy." Why was she defending him? She dismissed the thought. "But look at the diamonds on my finger, Honey. It's beautiful!" Emma was hurt, but didn't want to let her daughter know even though it appeared that Lyla knew exactly what she was feeling. They were about six years into the relationship, so she was happy that she got a ring, but she couldn't help but feel that she was robbed of what could have been a beautiful moment. Emma was not one to want *things*...all she wanted were moments with meaning. A diamond ring with no proposal meant nothing to her, so she knew that she would wait a long time before they would ever be married...if at all. But at least she didn't have to be embarrassed anymore, and could tell people at work and her family that she was engaged. People loved good news and they were all waiting for that moment just as much as she was. It was more difficult than she thought when people asked her how he proposed. She couldn't share with them the magical moment they were waiting to hear about. The only answer she could give was, "Oh, it was just so quick, but look how it sparkles!" She never had an answer for the obvious next question;

"When is the wedding?" She knew in her mind that the beautiful ring he had given her was simply a "shut up" ring. She wondered why Kyle and now Mitch didn't want to marry her...what was wrong with her?

THE DAY HE DIDN'T LOOK BACK

A few more years passed and they were getting ready to celebrate Lyla's 16th birthday with a big party. They looked at a few places until they found the perfect one that they knew Lyla would love.

"Mitch, it's just perfect! She is going to flip when she sees this, and the menu is amazing!" Mitch smiled. "It is Emma, everyone is going to be impressed. I have to invite all my friends to this party." Emma wasn't surprised that all he cared about was impressing people. She was just happy they could give Lyla this wonderful party that she deserved. After they closed the deal, they walked outside of the establishment, and Mitch said that he had a meeting that night and would see her the next day. Emma thought he would want to go to dinner or something with her especially after this special moment they were having, but he left. Emma noticed he didn't look back like he always did. They would wave at each other whenever they were heading to work or whatever it was, but this time, he never looked back. Emma thought that something was up...he seemed different.

About a week later they were home at Mitch's house where he was basically living now, and while he went to the store, she grabbed his laptop to look up sites for party invitations. His emails were open. When she went to close the page she noticed an email from a woman with the subject: "I love you." "It can't be!" Emma thought. Her heart started beating rapidly, she couldn't breathe, and her hands were numb. She looked a bit further and saw a lot more emails from the same woman. It was obvious by the content in the emails that Mitch was having an affair with this woman. Emma was crushed! She put the laptop down and just stared at it...she was shaking. She needed to know who this was and why he didn't just leave her to do what he wanted. iI he wasn't happy, he should just say so! Emma was furious! In a trance, she heard Mitch's voice as if it was a mile away.

"Hey, Honey...I got us some dinner. Do you want to sit outside or is it fine in here?" She couldn't move. She dealt with his temper and some of his crazy outbursts, but this? Why did he stay with her? He had freedom... she didn't get it. She thought what she had done to Kyle was coming back to haunt her. Was that why he wouldn't marry her...so he could cheat? She looked over at him and when he saw the look in her eyes, he put the food down.

"What?" He asked annoyedly. She went for it.

"Who is Irene?!" she asked sternly with a tremble in her voice. He looked at her and turned a bit pale. "Who?" Was he kidding? Was he really going to deny it? Then he seemed to catch on, and there was no hiding it. "Wait...are you looking at my emails?! he asked furiously.

"Do not change the subject! I went in to look for party invitations... your emails were up." She cried now. "What are you doing, Mitch? Who is this person? Why are you stringing me along? We are engaged! I trusted you. I thought you loved me, Mitch." She was crying uncontrollably. He went over to her but she pulled away. He put his hands on his hips and sighed, "It's nothing, Emma. I do love you. You are the love of my life. Nothing is going on." Emma stood up. "Nothing is going on? I had a beautiful evening with you, Irene? Can't wait to touch you again?! Mitch, try again." She was furious and hurt. "The emails are very graphic, you asshole!" she screamed at him. He looked sad and knew he couldn't hide this. She grabbed her bag and ran outside even though she had nowhere to go. She had no car and she was far from her apartment. Mitch followed.

"Emma, stop! Baby, please, let's talk." She kept walking. He caught up to her and turned her to him. They both stood there overwhelmed. She wondered what he was feeling...probably nothing, but he looked sad. Was he afraid to lose her after all, or was she just seeing things? Mitch knew he was wrong but he didn't want to lose her. He didn't know why, but he needed to get her back.

"Emma...Emma, please come inside! Let's talk...please, I'll explain." She looked at him with tears in her eyes and noticed tears in his. Although she wanted to keep going, her body was frozen...something held her back. "Move, Emma!" she told herself. Leave! She didn't. She wasn't ready to walk away.

"I'm sorry Emma! Please come home. I love you so much...I'm sorry. I didn't know where this was going, but I know now you're it for me. Please Honey, let's talk." She was so confused. She didn't know where this was going after so many years. Did it take men longer to settle, she wondered? The only reference Emma had was her dad, her pedophile grandfather, and Kyle. Mitch had given her more than any of them had.

She watched a grown man cry and she fell for it. It hurt her to see him like this. She thought maybe he was telling the truth...he sounded sincere. She was the only one he actually loved. It didn't completely make sense to her, but she felt comforted by it for some reason.

She wanted to hear his side of the story, so she took the hand he offered and went home with him. She had already alienated herself from everyone else, so she had no one to go to including her friend Tracey. They had been together for so long and raised Lyla together, however dysfunctional that was. She chose to give their relationship another try. Maybe this was the scare he needed to marry her. Emma had no idea about what love really was. This was it for her, and she was not ready to end this relationship.

"Let's go inside, Baby." What was she to do when the only person she 'thought' she had, was the person who was hurting her?

They stayed up all night talking and crying, trying to figure things out. She knew deep down...it didn't matter what excuses he made that night...he was wrong and she should leave. However, she also made up excuses that maybe he was right but unsure of their relationship. After all, she was not his wife yet, so what if he was confused?

After a long night of discussing their future, she decided to forgive him especially after his promise to marry her. This time she believed him. He was the only person she had in her life right now...she needed him.

THE MAN WITH MANY BUTTONS

Emma hoped that things would get back to normal after she forgave him for his betrayal, even though a little voice told her they wouldn't, she stayed. It only took a few days for her to realize that things wouldn't change. She didn't know if he was still having an affair, but the temper tantrums continued. They had less and less good moments, and more bad moments every week. Emma became more impatient and aware as time progressed, and Mitch seemed to get worse. It seemed like everything she did bothered him. Her loneliness grew, her sadness about not being strong for Lyla grew, and she missed her family. She was sensitive to everything. She felt she was losing herself more and more each day.

She knew it was time to fight to see her family, and she wondered how she let it get this far. He had an excuse or reason every time Emma brought up visiting her family. He would get mad and try to convince her that family members could not be trusted; like he was trying to brainwash her. They received an invitation from her sister, Sarah, who she had become estranged from. Sarah had a new baby and it was time that they reconciled. It was her fault for allowing Mitch to alienate them...she needed to fix it.

"Mitch, my niece is having a birthday party...let's go. It will be fun. I haven't met the baby yet and she just turned one." He was quick to react.

"Are you kidding me? A kid party?!" Mitch became enraged and went from zero to 100 in one second. "Wait! Why are you flipping out?" Emma was so angry. "Ugh! You get angry for no reason, Mitch. It's not normal." Mitch continued in his anger, "You don't love me, Emma. Why do you need other people?!! You don't need to go to any parties!!" Emma was stunned! She could never get used to his random, irrational outbursts. "Mitch! What is wrong with you? Stop screaming!! You are invited too, but you don't have to go. I will go with Lyla." She didn't care how he acted, she was going, but she noticed Lyla backing away slowly into her room as if to say, 'don't get me involved!' She was already giving up. Mitch's face contorted into an animalistic being as Emma fought back. He was scary to her. She knew that Lyla also felt like they were living with the devil himself. He would not let them be happy. He continued, "I'm your family! Are you saying I'm not enough? You don't love me, Emma!!" He became louder and louder as Emma stared at him. She didn't see the man she thought she knew and she felt scared. Something was off. She was angry with him but fearful at the same time. She continued to fight. She knew it didn't matter whether she went or not, he would still be angry, so this time she would go.

Even though she thought it might be a lost cause, she tried to reason with him. She had already allowed Lyla to see her weak and giving in even longer than she had with Kyle. She hoped it was not too late.

"Mitch, it's just for a baby...what's the big deal? Why are you so angry about it?!" "You are invited too. They are not excluding you." He wouldn't listen and screamed at her even more. Emma was so annoyed, she looked up to see if God was listening to all this mess. "Where are You?" she asked in her mind.

"Lyla!" he yelled out. Emma turned to Mitch, and felt her heart stop. Oh no, not Lyla! She needed to do something. Lyla was on the verge of a break down already since she started college.

"Lyla, come out here now. You want to go to this party?" She looked like she was five years old again, and shook her head no. Emma couldn't take the manipulation.

"Lyla, yes you do!" Lyla looked at her mother like she wanted her to be quiet. Emma knew her daughter wanted her to shut up and stop the fighting, but she also knew he wouldn't stop, and she decided to remain quiet no longer. She wondered why she couldn't give Mitch that same look since he was the crazy one. She knew it was because of fear, and that bothered her.

"See, she doesn't want to go. She agrees with me! Families are no good for us." Mitch stormed off, just like that - he'd won. His reactions and outbursts were becoming more frequent and abusive. Mitch came back into the den where Emma was sitting. She was crying out of frustration.

"You know, Emma, one day you will learn not to push my buttons!" He left the room again. Lyla had locked herself in her own room. Emma felt a fury come over her! She was so annoyed, she felt trapped, and she followed him into the kitchen.

"What does that even mean, 'buttons?' Are you kidding me?! That's what you say to me? You have buttons I push that make you abusive to me?!" Mitch was stunned since he had never seen Emma mad like that before. "Buttons, for a birthday party invite?! Are you insane?! And leave Lyla alone, do not yell at her!"

"I am not abusive, Emma. But you know what bothers me, so yeah you push my buttons and expect me not to react. I'm going to run away and hide in the mountains one day." What was he even talking about? He made no sense! She was so mad, she lunged at him crying hysterically! She'd had enough! As she tried to hit him, he looked afraid...surprised by it.

"Emma, stop!" he yelled out. She was so angry about everything that he snapped. Something stopped her and she backed away glaring at him. It was at that moment, she realized he was just a man, a coward...she was not fighting a man, but something sinister. She was sure she felt God pull her away, intervening. It took her a minute to calm her angry nerves.

"Wow, Emma. What was that?" She realized that he didn't even get why she was mad. She felt defeated. "You are crazy, Mitch? Everything bothers you - even a baby party. I'm sorry, but I can't do this - no matter what I do or want - you lose it. I mean, what are we doing? It's been 17 years and all we do is argue. I love you, but since I am with you, I am not myself. I don't have friends, I have pushed my family away, and I barely pray. You get upset by everything I do. I don't like who I am now and neither do you which you made very clear with Irene. I don't know why you are with me. Why can't you leave me be?!"

"Why would you bring that up? You said you forgave me!" he pleaded. "Oh Lord, make this stop," she said under her breath.

"Mitch, did you hear anything I said other than that?" Emma was beyond frustrated! She was being affected by him emotionally and felt like she was losing her mind. She stopped arguing and went to bed, although she couldn't sleep.

She couldn't wait to get to work. It had become her safe haven and she did well there - she felt normal. Emma knew there had to be a change in this relationship now 18 years in...too long. She might not have had the courage to leave him before because she was young and easily manipulated, but now she was feeling desperate and could finally see the possibility of being free. She realized a bit too late that there would be no wedding and no kids with him. She felt like she had blinders on...like he had put a spell on her or something where she didn't see what was going on. How did she not see it, she wondered? She had been targeted and controlled from day one. She had become submissive, and she never realized how much it all had affected her. So much happened throughout their lives together and she realized that "the light" that she once had, had dimmed. She lost herself along the way and she was becoming emotionally and physically ill. Something needed to be done.

WHAT IS NARCISSISM?

The next evening after work Emma went straight to her apartment. Mitch was not happy about it. "What do you mean you are home? This is your home...why are you there?!" Emma was tired of his attitude.

"Stop yelling at me, Mitch!" "I am not yelling and stop pressing my buttons, Emma. It's your fault...you went home." Did he think his behavior would make her want to be with him? She didn't have the energy to fight. She took the easy route and told him that she was sick. It wasn't completely a lie since she was emotionally exhausted.

"I don't feel well and I have an early morning at work. I'm staying here." Mitch hung up on her and Emma cried out of anger. Why was he so difficult? She never understood it. Still she was happy to be home...she needed a break. At that moment Lyla walked into the apartment. Emma's eyes lit up!

"Hi Honey, how was your day." Lyla noticed that her mom was crying, and decided to talk to her. "Mom, what's wrong? Is it Daddy?" Emma knew she couldn't hide anything from Lyla...she was now a grown woman. Emma smiled - she didn't want to poison her daughter by talking about Mitch, although Lyla already knew from her own experience.

"Mom, enough is enough!" Emma stood quietly. Lyla was never really verbal about anything...she wished she had been. "I'm so sad, Mom!" Lyla let out an uncontrollable loud cry...she couldn't stop. "Lyla, OMG! Honey, breathe!" She grabbed her daughter and let her release everything she was feeling.

"Why is he so crazy? I don't like when he yells at you and me - I can't take it! Why are you still with him?!" She sounded angry and depressed. All Emma could do was apologize and live with the guilt.

"I'm so sorry, honey. I don't know why I put up with it." Lyla continued, "Mom, I can't sleep, I am terrified every time he is home. I can't do this anymore - he makes me call him a million times a day and if I don't answer he gets so mad." Lyla cried hard and Emma held her tight. "What was happening?" she thought to herself. How did she get to this place? How could she allow anyone to treat her this way...especially her child? She didn't know who she was angrier with, Mitch or herself. Emma prayed in her mind, "God please help us. Why are you not intervening?!" She needed help. She knew what Lyla was saying was serious, and that she needed her and she needed help. She had been emotionally abused for years...ust like Emma.

She sat next to her daughter and held her there for a while apologizing as they both cried. "I am so sorry, Baby. I don't know how I allowed it to get this bad. I honestly don't understand myself. I don't know why I didn't stand up for you or me." Lyla loved her mother...she would help her because they needed each other.

"Mom, you were so young. He has been manipulating you all these years. He knew you were a single young mom...a perfect target for him. He promised you so much - even marriage and a baby. Me too, Mom... he's my dad, but I believed his lies too. I truly think there is more to it and he's worse than ever. Do you see it?" Emma knew that she was right.

"His behavior is horrible and I don't like how he mistreats you, Mom. I wish I had the courage to run away when I was younger because I'm scared all the time. It's like there is something wrong with his mind." Emma felt the tears welling up.

"Oh Honey, run away? I don't know why I didn't have the courage to." "Mom, listen...I did some research." Emma looked at her beautiful daughter. "Research?!" Emma was confused.

"Yes, mom there is so much information on people like Daddy." "People like Daddy? What was she talking about?" Emma thought. "I mean - I guess I always knew his behavior wasn't normal. I didn't see it right away. He was kind in the beginning. He just always blamed it on being Italian." Lyla grabbed her laptop.

"Mom, look here is one option: BPD (Borderline Personality Disorder). Dad has all the traits. Then there is Bipolar too, but I think it's this: 'Narcissism,' which is definitely more like him - or both. I don't know, but Mom - it's something like this." Emma turned the laptop towards her.

"Let me see this. The Mayo Clinic describes it as: 'Narcissism', a mental condition in which people have an inflated sense of their own importance, a deep need for excessive attention and admiration, troubled relationships, and a lack of empathy for others. They attack and abuse anyone who they feel, makes them look bad or if they feel unloved."

"Oh, my word!" Emma couldn't believe what she was reading. It was a complete description of Mitch...she was shocked! She couldn't deny the guilt she felt that her daughter did her own research to figure out what was wrong with her father.

"Lyla, no wonder. Honey...I don't know what I have to do but I will try something. I am so sorry Baby...so sorry I dragged you into this relationship. I don't think I could ever make it up to you, but things are going to change. It's the least I can do to try to improve our lives. Please forgive me, Lyla. How could this happen? Why did I let it happen?" Emma sobbed. Now it was her daughter who consoled her.

"Mom, it's okay. We should be happy. At least I'm going back to college, but you need to do something about this. According to all of this information, and Dad's behavior, he will never change, and it is not your job to fix him. Mom, I think first we both need to see someone professional...a therapist maybe." Emma agreed and they hugged.

"When did you become the adult between us, Lyla? I'm so proud of you." Emma promised to find help for the both of them through her insurance. They finally felt a little hope.

Emma didn't sleep much that evening thinking about what Lyla told her. She needed to figure something out. She just wished that she had done it while Lyla was still a child. It's never too late, she thought.

Mitch called Emma at work the next day. "Emma, are you coming over tonight? I need you to help me pack. I have a business trip tomorrow morning." Emma knew he didn't need helping packing one suit for this trip, but she humored him. She had unfinished business with Mitch and didn't know yet how she would break up with him after all these years. She agreed that she would go, but with the intention to pack some stuff of her own to bring back to her apartment - she just didn't share that part. Then again, she knew it might be an excuse...she was still afraid to leave him. It wouldn't be easy. He surely would not make it easy for her to leave.

When she arrived at the home they shared for so many years, she knew she would miss it. Despite the arguing and crazy moments, there were some good moments sprinkled in, like when they entertained by hosting parties and dinners for friends. They had built this home together, unfortunately for them, it was dysfunctional. Unfortunate for her - she didn't know the difference - her whole life was dysfunctional.

Emma looked up at the sky. It was starting to get dark and she prayed, "God, help me please. I don't know what I am walking into, but I need you to follow me. Help me figure out what to do." She was starting to realize that Mitch might be someone that she couldn't handle alone. Kyle was difficult, but Mitch had a whole other dimension. She walked in and found him in the kitchen.

"Hey Honey, you hungry? I got Chinese food and we can watch a movie..." Emma looked at him - what was happening?

"Don't you have to pack? You have a very early flight." She knew he would be up all night trying on suit after suit - he did that often. She just didn't feel like watching him do it. "Nah, I can do it later. Let's order food and watch a movie that I like." He meant they would watch a movie that she hated.

THE RUNNER

Remembering how they met was a far cry from where they were now and she didn't know how to handle it or what to do. She had to come up with a plan to figure it out and there was no turning back now. It was the only way she felt strong enough right now at least, to leave him, or to figure out if that was what she really wanted. The last time that she was in a similar situation, she left Kyle a note. She didn't like running, hiding, or not facing situations, but she didn't know what else to do. Would Mitch lose it?

She arrived at the hotel near the airport and checked in... relieved and excited. Thankfully, her room was very quiet. She breathed in the silence that she so desperately needed and prayed for strength.

"Well…" she said out loud, "Here I am." She looked at her cell phone in fear...hoping Mitch wouldn't call. He was always busy on his business trips, but you never knew with Mitch. She ordered room service, but could barely eat, so she called the front desk for a wakeup call for her early flight and for car service to the airport, and went to bed. The excitement and stress kept her awake, and she worried about Mitch's reaction when he found out, but eventually she fell asleep from exhaustion.

The next morning the phone in the hotel room rang and Emma jumped up not remembering where she was for a moment. Perhaps it was

Mitch, but then she realized that he didn't know that she was there, so it couldn't possibly be him. She picked up the phone and she was right...it was her wakeup call. She quickly got ready, went to the hotel lobby, checked out, and jumped into the cab she had reserved. She was nervous but excited, and couldn't believe she was doing this. "What am I doing?" she asked herself. She smiled to herself and looked at her phone with butterflies in her stomach. She was tempted to leave her cell phone behind,but just couldn't allow herself to cut all ties with Mitch just yet. A talk with him about what she was feeling and what her plans were would have to happen. At the moment, she really didn't feel like doing anything...she wanted to just leave. As she reached the airport and was getting her bags out of the cab, her phone rang and this time it was Mitch...she froze! After taking a deep breath, she paid the driver and walked into the airport lobby before answering. She took another deep breath. "Hello," she said softly. "Hey, are you not at work? I called you?" he asked, apparently annoyed. She answered quickly hoping he wouldn't hear anything that would indicate she was at the airport. "No, I wasn't feeling well so I called in sick." Emma wasn't ready to deal with him just yet. Mitch accepted her response and hung up.

Although the call made her nervous, she felt good and in control of her steps. It had been a very long time since she felt that good about any decision she had made. She grabbed her bag and walked towards her gate. Once she got through security, she sat down to wait for her flight and felt nervous again. She decided to just deal with the stress she was feeling, so she could enjoy her alone time. She wrote him an email.

The message began with "I love you," because she thought she did. It also said that she wasn't well emotionally and needed to focus on that. She needed time to herself to figure things out. Whether he would understand or not, she was still leaving, and she wanted to be honest with him.

Once she sent that email, he would immediately call her, so it was good that she was at the airport where he couldn't talk her out of it. It took about 10 minutes before he made that call. Emma picked up ready to deal with him, but she said a quick prayer first.

"Hi," was all she said, knowing exactly why he was calling.

"Emma, what are you doing?" he asked surprisingly calmly. "I didn't know you were feeling this way...why didn't you come to me?" He really was delusional in that he didn't accept the fact that he was the cause of her anxiety.

"Mitch, I need to do this - I need to go home. I'll be back, but I need some time to myself." Mitch was not happy but remained calm.

"So, you don't talk to me...you run away?" She remained silent. Her mind was made up and she knew he wouldn't understand. "Okay," he said. "Can you at least call me when you get there so I don't worry?" She accepted that and pretended that he cared.

"Yes, I will call you when I land, because I know you worry, but after that we will talk when I return." He sighed.

"Emma, don't do this. Honey, I love you...please." He tried to change her mind, just like she knew he would. "I love you too, Mitch, but I need some time alone. I'll call you later. I have to board now." She hung up.

Emma boarded the plane and all she could think about was her family. Happy that Mitch was aware, she could now just relax and enjoy her family. She said another prayer because at this point, it was evident that she could not pull this off on her own...she needed God.

With the money she had saved up she flew first class. If she was going to do this, then she was going to do it right! She didn't work hard for nothing. She felt the tiredness seep in and she let it come. It didn't take long for her to doze off since she hadn't slept in days.

When she opened her eyes, Mitch was sitting next to her...staring at her with anger in his eyes, shaking her shoulders. Suddenly, Emma woke up frightened, but then realized it wasn't Mitch.

"Ma'am…!" Someone was shaking her arm. The flight attendant woke her up because they had landed. She couldn't believe she fell asleep for the entire trip, and felt relief...she was home. She could not wait to get off the plane, so she grabbed her carry on and walked to the baggage claim area to get her other bag. While waiting for her bag to arrive, Emma searched for her dad's face in the crowd of people. She looked back and saw her bag right in front of her. She grabbed it and left the baggage claim area.

She could not believe she managed this escape, but she pulled it off. It sucked, she thought, that she had to go this extreme, but she felt there was no other way.

Her cell phone showed a missed call from Mitch, but she couldn't be bothered with it...not right now.

"Emma!" She heard her dad's voice calling her...she searched for him. "Emma... over here!" She saw his terrific smile as he waved at her. He was as handsome as ever...she ran to him. "Dad!" She ran into his arms and couldn't hold back the tears. She wanted to stay there forever...she felt so safe.

"You're home, Baby." He held her tightly. Emma relaxed her hug and looked at her dad's tearful face. He looked a little older but healthy otherwise. He had changed. She knew he had, and was so happy about it. They smiled and went on their way. As soon as Emma walked outside of the terminal, she enjoyed the scent of the Caribbean that filled the air, and felt the hot sun shine on her face. Boy, did she miss this...the simple things in life! She took a deep breath and took it all in.

"There is nothing like the ocean breeze lingering in the air, Dad. I missed home so much!" At that moment her phone rang and it was Mitch. She stopped where she was, texted him back quickly that she had landed safely, and put her phone away.

"Work?" Her dad stopped...he knew his daughter too well. "No," she answered as she gave him a smile, and he put his hand on her arm. "Emma, if you are not happy you must do something about it." She should have known she couldn't hide anything from him. "I don't want to upset you, but you didn't even let us celebrate your engagement," he said. The "fake engagement," she thought. Her dad continued, "You haven't shared your life with us. I'm just worried about it all. We can talk about this later...just know that if you need me for anything, I am here." He smiled at her, and she knew he was right.

"Thanks, Dad but...." She started to lie but only the truth came out.

"You're right...I'm not happy. My engagement was not even real. He handed me a ring and didn't even propose. I waited, but he didn't ask me to marry him. How am I supposed to take that?" She cried... "I feel like he doesn't truly love me. There is something wrong with how he acts, Dad. I don't know how I could be so blind. I don't understand any of it." Her dad held her tightly as she looked up at him. "I ran away, Dad." Her dad's eyes widened and she cried some more.

"What? He doesn't know you are here?" he asked worriedly. "I only told him when I was at the airport. It was the only way, Dad." He looked at her and turned her towards him. "Is he hurting you? Is he abusive?" Emma's eyes widened.

"Not the way you think...not with his hands, but yes. It's okay Dad...I'm home and I am going to enjoy this." He replied, "God sent you here. He's been waiting for you, Honey. You don't have to go through this alone, why are you trying to?" He smiled at his daughter and gently wiped her tears. "Let's go home."

As they drove away from the airport, her heart was filled with joy. She had her dad, her family, the food she loved, and the ocean breeze... it was all she ever wanted. The simple things in life satisfied her. She would exchange all of Mitch's money, trips, clothes, watches, purses, and everything just to be happy. It was a lesson that perhaps she had to learn. They drove through San Juan...a place dear to her heart. They passed over the bridge where there were tons of Puerto Rican flags, and she smiled. Her dad enjoyed watching his daughter take in the sights. He saw how excited she was looking at everything. He wondered what her life was like now. She had distanced herself from everyone, but he never intervened. It was her life, but he knew she would be back. He just wanted to hold on to these moments they had until she left again.

"We will eat at home. I have something special cooked up for you. Before that, is there anything you want to do?" He smiled because he knew the answer. She turned to him and asked, "Can we stop by the ocean for a second?" "Of course!" He took her to 'Condado' near San Juan, and 'Santurce,' since it was the closest to where they were. They got out of the car and Emma walked towards the ocean and stood there just glancing at it as if it spoke to her. She closed her eyes and prayed quietly to give thanks. Once she felt that she had her fill, they left to head home. She couldn't wait to see everyone, but she didn't know they would already be at her dad's house.

Her brother, David was anxiously waiting for her. He had become a pastor and she was beyond proud of him. He was there with his wife and kids. Her sister, Raquel was also there anxiously waiting with her kids. They pulled up to her father's house and it was just like she left it. She felt like she wanted to cry because she missed it so much.

"I'll get those bags for you, Honey. You go on up." Emma just stood there for a minute, soaking up the sun, and watched the one palm tree that stood in front of the house as it swayed slowly in the breeze. She turned her face to the sky, closed her eyes, and gave thanks again.

"Thank you, God, for this. Thank you, for giving me the courage to take this step and come back home." She felt her heart being mended just a little.

Emma followed her father. As soon as she reached the stairs, the aroma of her dad's cooking filled the air. He opened the door and let Emma go in first. She walked in and was surprised to see everyone there. It was a very emotional moment. She couldn't believe that she had waited so long for this. She ran into her brothers' arms. He was so tall, but still a little brother to her. He cried as soon as he saw her. Then she realized she felt even more guilt than she anticipated. How could she stay away for so long? How could she do this to her family, and how could she keep them away from her daughter? She felt angry and disappointed in herself. All of this because of one man! She felt somewhat ashamed and realized she had not been this happy in years.

Dad interrupted her lingering thoughts. "You ready to eat, Emma?" he asked. "Is that a trick question, Dad?!" she asked happily. They sat and ate, they shared stories, and they sang while her dad played the guitar like they always had done in the past. She sang a duet with her dad, and then the family joined in. The room was filled with love and she missed it dearly. She couldn't believe she had stayed away from this happy and peaceful environment. She promised herself she would never stay away too long ever again. She needed this. It had confirmed what had taken her so long to realize...she was not happy and was not with the right man. What her daughter discovered about his personality resonated…"narcissism" made a lot of sense. Not only did he care only about himself and how he looked, he was also abusive in so many ways. Her brother, David approached her. "So, Emma I know you've been going through a lot, but know that we are here for you...we have always been." Emma knew.

"While you are at it, my church is having a three day retreat this weekend and I think you should go. It is last-minute, but I can get you in." At first Emma wasn't sure because she just wanted to be with her family, visit a spa, and hit the beach like the old days, as much as she could. She was going to say no, but she thought of the strength God gave her to be where she was at this moment. "I could really use a lot more of that," she thought.

"Okay fine, David...sign me up." Her brother smiled. The family talked about how they had all attended this retreat and it gave them a new awakening. "What are the odds that I am here at the very moment that there is a retreat?" she asked herself. She knew she should do it especially after checking her phone and seeing 3 missed calls and 10 text messages from Mitch.

She decided to call him because she was annoyed that he was blowing up her phone! Having her family there also made her feel empowered. He answered on the first ring.

"Where are you?!" he asked in a very loud voice. There was no greeting, just a loud, "where are you." "I told you where I would be, Mitch. I'm at my dad's." she answered calmly.

"Are you sure, Emma?" Doubting her made her furious. "What are you trying to say, Mitch? You are the one who cheated...there is no reason for you to think that of me." He dropped it, and asked, "When are you coming home?" She tried to sound confident. "When I am ready, and please do not call me or text me...this is not helping." He was silent for a few moments. "Okay, I'm sorry you're right, Emma. I'm just worried about you."

"You don't need to be worried, Mitch. I'll be fine. I'm with my family. Also, I will be attending a retreat at church and won't be able to use my phone, so give me a few days to call you." Mitch felt a little fear not knowing where Emma would be.

"Okay, Emma...just be careful. I'm sorry you are feeling this way. I know you have been through a lot in your life. I will be here when you get back." He hung up.

"How could he be so oblivious?" she thought. How could he think that he doesn't have anything to do with how she felt? She turned off the ringer...after all, everyone she wanted to talk to and needed were in one room. She couldn't help the upset stomach, but for the first time in their relationship she felt happy. She stood up for herself this time and she felt proud of that. Whatever he said just did not matter at that point. She needed to be incontrol of her life, and never realized when or how she gave it up in the first place. Then there was the cheating and the emotional abuse of her and daughter. How did she ever put up with all of that, she wondered? God teaches us to respect others, and to be respected...this was not what Mitch wanted for her, or for anyone else.

WAKE UP CALL

Emma was nervous about the weekend of the retreat. She had no idea what it was about other than it would be her and a bunch of other people trying to connect with God. At least, that's what she thought it was about. Her fear was that she would go back home without having the tools to deal with her life. She was intimidated not knowing anyone there, but there was something she needed...she just didn't know what it was, but hoped she would find it there.

"Well David, all I know is I need something. I'm not okay, my life is not okay, and I seem to have made every bad choice I could throughout adulthood." David gave his big sister a hug and reassured her. "Emma, when we don't' know what to do, or what we are feeling, or even what we need, God is the answer." With that he sent Emma off. Emma carried tons of emotional baggage, and hoped that God would show up and get rid of some of it for her.

When she arrived, she felt out of her element, but felt safe at the same time. The retreat was meant to be a 'one-on-one' with God, so there would be no outside connection. It was strange, and probably needed for Emma since Mitch was glued to her life in person and via phone. There were about 40 people or so, some of whom were married couples. It was nice to see that many people are working on fixing their lives by connecting the only true way - through God.

"Okay, Emma… focus! It's time to think, forgive, love, remember, pray, and worship Him." What Emma did not realize was how much she needed time alone. Perhaps being away from such a toxic, controlling person like Mitch made it easy. This experience, at this time in her life, was what she needed...a personal encounter with God.

After the retreat, Emma's family met her at church. During lunch she shared her experience with them.

"David, it was amazing. Thank you for fitting me in. I knew while growing up that God existed...I mean, jeez - you and I were at church just about 3 to 4 times a week, but I never understood how reachable He is. He is my God and I can talk to Him, ask Him for help, cry to Him, and thank Him for everything He has done for us." David smiled and hugged his sister. She loved him so much. She really didn't want to share with him her experience of forgiving their grandfather, since David had a different and good relationship with him. Unfortunately, their grandfather had everything to do with distorting her view of God. The retreat provided a good healing lesson on that subject too.

She felt enlightened, new, fresh, and protected and it gave her strength. It was also extremely difficult because she had to face reality...her reality.

"Raquel, I'm so embarrassed...I put Mitch before God. I didn't realize how much of me I had given to this guy...so much that I even forgot about myself. I never really talked to God too much - Mitch became my center."

Raquel shared some stories of her own with her big sister. "I'm sorry I left Raquel. Whatever the reasons - however valid, I'm sorry. I love you, and I miss you and David terribly. I literally abandoned all of you because of this man. How could I let that happen?" Her sister held her tightly, and they cried together. It had been a long time coming.

Spending time away from Mitch and with her family instead, became a crucial moment in her life...a wakeup call. "Dad, I am so sad." They hugged. "It's okay, Honey. You needed this...we all needed this...for you to come home and all of us to be together." She might still be a bit attached to Mitch since they had spent so many years together, but she was surely learning about how bad all of it was, and she wanted to get out of it. The old thought of puzzle pieces covering her body from the bottom up...

very close to covering completely, came to mind. It was time to work on removing those puzzle pieces entirely this time and let her light shine. Figuring out what each puzzle piece meant in order to remove it, would require work, but would be so worth it.

"I can do it this time, Dad. I learned God is with us always and everywhere. There were so many times I demanded He show up, especially when Mitch and I were fighting, but He was there. All I needed to do was take action and leave. I hope I can do that now." She had hit rock bottom and she knew it, so this retreat actually came at the perfect time... it was meant for her. God had given her the strength she asked for to leave Mitch behind in order to find herself and to be reminded of how much God loved her.

She learned about forgiveness, and how not only did she have to be forgiven, but also, she had a list of people she needed to forgive. Once she gave her brother David the okay, she made up her mind to give her all to the retreat and to surrender to God. She needed His help.

"Guys, I still have unfinished business at home, but these few days I spent focusing only on the goodness of Jesus, prepared me for what's to come. I have a lot of thinking to do, and changes to make, but I promise, Dad, I will never stay away for this long ever again!" He smiled.

"Don't think about any of that. You just had an amazing experience with God...don't taint it. Follow only Him. He will tell you what to do, if you let Him." She knew her father was right. "And you better not stay away for too long! I love you, Baby! God bless you on your journey."

She would enjoy her family for the remainder of the vacation and return home to figure things out...there was no time like the present. She told Mitch she would not be returning home to deal with anything until she was ready. He was not to pick her up from the airport either...he agreed. She had bigger plans for her life, and he was no longer going to be a part of it. She was starting to feel hopeful.

Her sister, Raquel, took her aside. She wanted sister time. "Just remember Emma, it's always easy when you are filled with the Holy Spirit to do anything. Don't let it wear off! If it does, try to bring it back with faith and praying. I know Mitch...I have seen how he has treated you and he is a strong character." Emma knew she was right, but she would think about that later. "I love you, Sis. I'm sorry again for staying away. I didn't really see what was happening to me, but then I started to notice little things and there we were 18 years in." Raquel smiled at her. "Don't worry about that now - tomorrow we are headed to the beach!" "Oh yes!" Emma thought...the ocean gave her peace.

NOT FOREVER AFTER

When she landed at the airport, she felt strange since she usually traveled with Mitch, but she was confident and perfectly fine about getting her own cab and going home on her own. While sitting in the cab she started to think about the list of goals and accomplishments she had written a week earlier...all the things she wished she could do but hadn't. Those were things she needed to catch up on.

She felt good about getting home to a quiet place that was all hers. When she arrived home, she called Mitch. He answered at the first ring.

"Oh, thank God, you're safe!" He sounded agitated. "Why wouldn't I be safe?" She simply said, "Yes, I landed fine and I'm home now." She added, "Mitch, we need to talk." The line was quiet for a few seconds.

"Emma, come home after work tomorrow. Please, Honey,I need to see you." Emma agreed since she wanted to pick up some things and tell him she was taking a break. She felt strong.

Emma was happy to return to work, and it felt good not having to report back to Mitch every second of the day; things were different now. She had a lot to catch up on and needed to focus. She was there for herself and her career which she cherished. It was important for her to do well.

When her shift was over, she went to the house to deal with whatever was to come. He looked defeated. Act 1 began. He looked like he had aged overnight, or perhaps it was because she had been around so much positivity in the last week that she saw him for who he really was. He greeted her with a kiss and he held her close. "Should we have dinner?" he asked.

"I'm not that hungry...I'll have something light." She felt awkward because he was being nice. They sat and ate, but Emma knew they needed to talk although it appeared that he did't want to. "Mitch…" she started when he interrupted.

"Emma, let's just relax tonight okay? We can talk tomorrow. I'm just glad you are home, and I got you some bathing suits for our next trip." She looked at him in disbelief, and felt her heart beat faster. She loved him still, but why, she wondered? She thought about what her sister, Raquel said about the joyfulness wearing off. It started to happen. When he was nice it was very difficult for her to say no to him. "My gosh," Emma thought, "I was so strong just a few days ago."

She decided to stay with him a few days, to see if she could maybe leave him less abruptly than she had originally planned. She felt a tug as if she was already making wrong choices, but she also knew that she was ready to leave him on her own terms and time. She felt that there would never be a good time, and since they had a trip planned, how could she cancel?

"Ugh, I need my family to help me, but God - I know you are here! Please give me strength to handle whatever this is."

The next morning Emma got ready for work. She went to the kitchen to make coffee when Mitch came down to greet her.

"Emma, I'm working from home today. Why don't you stay?" She looked at his handsome face and realized that by giving him a scare he was acting differently towards her. She wondered how long it would last...did he really change? Perhaps he learned his lesson, she thought.

"Mitch, I really need to go in. I've been out for a week, but I'll be back after work." She kissed him goodbye and went on her way. She felt in control this time, but it made her nervous that it might not last. The tools that were given to her at the retreat, and being closer to God made her stronger. She would pray for them both. She didn't want to give up on all of the years they had together. She thought it would be better with her new found faith and strength. She would try to share that joy with Mitch. She liked this version of Mitch, and if he continued to be nice like this, perhaps she would give it a try. Maybe it wasn't narcissism...maybe he just needed help...or maybe she was too afraid to leave, she wondered. The bigger question was, why?

"Emma, if you gain more weight, how can I love you?" They were having a discussion about love and what it meant one afternoon, and he shocked her with his crude comment. "Mitch, I'm a size 5 now...I'm not fat. What are you talking about?" He was the one who gained weight, but she didn't care. It was like he was projecting how he saw himself onto her.

"No, but I met you when you were thin, so you have to stay thin." Gosh, she hated him sometimes! Mitch might not be a physical abuser, but the emotional and verbal abuse was just as horrifying. She had developed an eating disorder a few years back and it just hit her...maybe he was the trigger. It didn't surprise her that Mitch would go back to his old self either, but she chose to give him the benefit of the doubt. He was very convincing and charming when he wanted something from her, but she learned a little too late that the goodness in him was an act...the real Mitch was a selfish man.

"Why don't you find someone skinny then?" she said to him. "Like that girl Irene... I know you are seeing her again, or maybe it never even stopped." Mitch got angry.

"That's not true!" Emma knew it was true. She heard him talking on the phone with her. "Mitch, why don't you just leave so you can date whoever you want?" Mitch turned to her. "Emma, I know I have cheated before, but I love only you." She couldn't believe he had the audacity to say that and to even think that any of what he was saying made sense. "So, let me see if I understand this...you have cheated on me, but you love only me." He then yelled at her.

"Yeah, yeah, I love only you! You are young and beautiful, and sometimes I can't believe you are with me, so I have cheated because I didn't want you to have the edge." Wow, she thought! She could not believe what he was saying and that he thought it was okay to feel that way. At least now she knew how he felt, but still neither one of them had the guts to break it off, so it got dragged out for a long time. They had become co-dependents. She had been with him since she was 25 years old, and now she was in her late 40's. It was a bit terrifying because she was so emotionally dependent on him, and for years, all she heard from him was about how she wouldn't be able to survive without him. The talk about weight turned into an argument.

"You won't be able to live without me! You will see how broke you really are, and how little you have, Emma."

"What? Why are you talking about money? Is that the hold you think you have on me?" She had a job and didn't need things the way that he did, but she still feared being alone. "I have never been a materialistic person, Mitch. I have never asked for anything from you." Emma knew he was getting more out of her than she was of him, and was 100% sure that she wanted nothing from him anymore. She wondered where her strength disappeared to... she needed to leave again.

One Sunday, late afternoon, Lyla was home on break. They had an early dinner together at the table, and Mitch began what had become routine at this point...interrogating Lyla. The usual would happen...Emma would defend her daughter...Lyla would ask her not to because then they would argue, and Lyla would end up crying. Emma was tired of walking on eggshells to avoid an argument. He deserved to be argued with, and she needed to express herself.

"So, Lyla, how's the expensive college education I am paying for?" Emma looked at him in disbelief. She was the one who was paying for her college. He had not paid a dime yet, but was supposed to pay Emma back and pick up the payments from there. He had told Lyla that she could attend any university she wanted, and he would gladly pay for as long as she went. Lyla had her mind set on college since she was little, but never thought she would attend a university far from them, but now she needed to for her own emotional wellbeing. She never intended to come back, and Emma supported her.

"You know, just because you are away at college doesn't mean you get to do whatever you want. You have to call me as soon as you get up and when you leave for class, and call me when you get home and before bed too." Emma interrupted his ridiculous demands. "Mitch, do we have any plans with Lyla since we made her come home? We should do something special since we don't get to see her often." Surprise, surprise - Mitch got angry! "She's home, Emma. What do you mean,plans? No...no plans, and stop texting whoever that is." Lyla was furious and looked at Emma as if to say, "don't intervene!" Emma couldn't hold her tongue. She no longer respected the man she once had on a pedestal.

"Mitch, stop...just stop! She just got home. We are supposed to enjoy her, not make her want to leave. She can text whoever she wants...she's an adult! Can't you see how miserable she is?" He gave Emma a nasty look and the fight started. Lyla began to cry, and got up to leave the room.

"Where are you going?!" he demanded! She sat back down. Mitch had so much control that Emma couldn't comprehend it. His voice and words were like daggers that paralyzed their emotions. "Listen to me," he said in a scary low voice. "I'm done!" His voice got louder. "I'm done with everything...with trying to please you both, with the lack of respect, with all of the secrets, and one of these days I'll be gone and no one will know where I am." "Secrets?" Emma thought to herself.

He continued with his rant. "I can no longer do this with you guys making me the bad guy. All I do is spend my money on you and try to make you happy. Family is no good! You can't trust your family! Everything here I earned...it's mine! No one loves me...you guys don't love me. You will see how horrible the world is without me! You are a bitch, and Lyla is not far behind. I give you everything including my life, and all you want to do is hurt me! 'F' you! 'F' youuuu!" His screams felt like a million punches all over her body and she would never get used to his cursing and verbal abuse. She felt like he was destroying her from the inside out. Lyla knew her mother was paying for college even though he promised her that he would pay for her to go to any good university she wanted. He was not truthful in anything he said. The more he talked the louder and scarier he became, and he went on for another hour. Emma felt herself getting physically ill, and she knew Lyla was feeling the same thing. Lyla went to her room after he was finally done.

"Emma, leave her be! Stay down here with me." She refused and promised herself that she would never do that again. She went to her daughters' room. "Lyla, Honey..." Emma could see the look on Lyla's face... it scared her. "I hate him! He's evil, Mom. Why did I even come home?!" Emma knew that she was right, and this made her want to leave even more. "I'm so sorry, Baby! I don't know what hold he had on me. I can't believe I am still here and that I subjected you to him." Lyla hugged her mom and said, "'Mom, you never told me that he cheated on you." Emma was surprised to hear Lyla say that, but she would no longer protect him. "I heard you say it when you were arguing." Emma sighed. "Yes, he did Lyla - many times. He still is. Please don't look at me that way...I don't understand it either." Lyla looked at her with anger in her eyes. "What?! Mom, are you serious? " Emma's shame was visible as she carried it on her shoulders along with guilt. "I'm leaving for good, Lyla." Lyla rolled her eyes...she didn't believe her. "You already did, and came right back."

"I know...he won't let me be...I'm scared sometimes. I needed to build up enough courage to finally be on my own." Lyla understood that part. "Praying and having faith has built a strength in me that I never knew one could have. My mind...my thoughts were gone from this relationship long ago, Lyla. I know God has big plans for me, and I have learned this year that the enemy doesn't want me to fulfil those plans. So, I am putting my faith in God and I am ready to leave." Lyla was quiet. "That ridiculous tantrum from a narcissist is much more than that. It's evil and it will be the last time he speaks to any of us like that. Lyla, I won't see Mitch anymore. It's scary and that is a battle we cannot fight. Daddy is God's son just like we are His daughters. I'm giving Daddy to God to handle. I cannot and should not try to handle him." Lyla cried. She didn't know why since she wasn't very spiritual, but for some reason she believed her mother this time.

"I failed you...I am so sorry. Everything is going to change. I can see he is not well, and since he won't seek help, I have to leave him. We are already both sick all the time, Lyla, with all this stress that he puts us through. It is time to take care of us, like you said...we need professional help."

"Listen to me, Hon. You have plans with a friend tomorrow, yes?" Lyla nodded.

"If Dad doesn't stop me." Emma grabbed her daughter's hands.

"You will go. I don't care how angry he gets and tries to stop you. You pack your bag right now! Tomorrow, when your friend comes to pick you up, you leave. On Sunday, you go back to school. I will have a ticket ready for you...do you understand?!" Lyla never saw her mother this way... she seemed determined. "Really? You will let me go?" Emma hugged her daughter as she cried. Letting her go was the only good thing she could do for her.

"Mom, what about you? You already left him, but came back." Emma smiled. "I have a plan too. I don't want you to think about it, so pack your things and go to bed. I will come in the morning to say goodbye." She kissed her daughter's forehead. "Te amo! God bless you, Baby."

"Mom, I wish you had done this earlier in my life, but I am glad you are doing it now. I know you can't fight this and neither can I."

Guilt was on her list of things to overcome, but God promised He would be there for her, so she was going to take Him up on it. She would be okay on her own, because God was with her. She was starting to understand the reasons why this man had so much control over her as she became closer to God. The enemy wanted to continue to rule her life, but Emma would no longer allow it. God was in control now. She had been afraid and insecure, but God made her stronger every day, and the stronger she became, the more she saw the evil in Mitch, and the damage that he was doing to her and Lyla. The enemy was whispering in her ear, playing with her mind through Mitch for years. Emma had enough. God had freed her! "Ephphatha," He said to her and she saw the full truth. "Lord, thank you for opening up my senses. Help me now to leave, protect me from him, and help Lyla as well."

Mitch didn't say much to Lyla the next morning, because he liked her friend and was talking to him about computer stuff. When they were on their way, Emma gave Lyla a wink and blew her a kiss. Her time would come in the morning when Mitch went to visit his mother, another person who he also kept distanced from Emma. She no longer cared...she was out of there!

She prayed hard that night. She needed every ounce of faith she could muster. "Mitch, I'll be out in a minute. I'm going to take a shower and I'll be down." She needed a few minutes away from Mitch to execute her plan while Mitch watched a football game on TV. "Okay, Hon. Make me some tea after?"

"Sure," she answered then ran to the master bath, logged on to her phone, and clicked on the 'United Airlines' app. She bought a ticket and didn't care about the last-minute cost. She was going back home to Puerto Rick again. It had already been a year since she had been home. She could not believe that she had put herself through another year with Mitch. This was a serious issue that needed to be addressed.

Emma knew she was running again, but she didn't know what else to do. It was like she told her friend Tracey, "Breaking up isn't like in the movies, Tracey. I am not in the movie, 'Sleepless in Seattle' when she breaks up with her boyfriend and he just agrees, or in, 'You've Got Mail' where they both agree the relationship wasn't working, and they're both fine with it. I am dealing in real life with a man who I don't know what he will do...a man I am scared of."

Runner or not, Emma took action. This time she would leave for good. She showered, packed a little bag, made Mitch some tea, and went to bed.

FREEDOM

"Okay, Emma... going to Mom's. I might take her to lunch, so I'll see you later tonight." Perfect, she thought. She would have time to pack a bigger bag and get a cab without any worries. This time, she sent Mitch an email about her leaving when she arrived at 'Luis Munoz Marin International airport' in San Juan, Puerto Rico. He immediately called her. He was angry with her, but not surprised this time.

"You act like I had other options. You won't let me leave, Mitch. I knew you would try to stop me. I had to leave this way. Why would you want me to stay anyway, Mitch? You have Irene, and I do not need to, nor will I put up with that anymore?" Mitch paused on the phone.

"Emma, I love you. You are it for me. Once you sign the prenuptial agreement, we can get married." Too late for that, she thought. What was it with the men in her life who only proposed to her when she decided to finally leave them? "No!" she thought...not this time. There was no way that Emma could survive another day with Mitch, let alone get married to him, which she knew was only another tactic to make her come back.

He tried to convince her, but she already knew legally, what would not happen. "Mitch, I have been in this relationship for 20 years of my life. You gave my daughter your name, we have accounts together, and I have given up everything for you already. Why would you ever think I would sign a prenup...for what? I am already in it! I have been for basically my whole adult life. What could that prenup possibly say that I have not already survived with you?!" Emma was angry that he would even mention it at this point in their relationship.

"Well, it would say something like, if you leave me in 5 years you get whatever amount or nothing depending on the reason." She was amazed at his audacity!

"Really, Mitch?! And what about the nearly 20 I have already survived, your abusiveness, your cheating, you pretending to love me, your pretending to pay for college?" She was furious! He was the cheater, the liar and the abuser. Was he kidding? He laughed at her comments.

"Why are you laughing, Mitch? This is serious." He laughed a little more. "Because I love you! Boy, have I created a monster! You are right. So, will you please give up the apartment so we can begin our lives together?" He truly was insane if he thought that after 20 years they would be *starting* their lives together.

"That doesn't sound like a proposal, Mitch. Please leave me be! We are not good for each other." Mitch cried on the phone and Emma knew it was fake. Every time she gave in to him, he would fight with her over nothing, again and again. She told Mitch that it was over, and chose to enjoy her vacation and family time.

"Dad, I need church. I know God is everywhere, but I feel him here more than anywhere else." Her dad laughed. He knew what she meant.

After service, her family got together and they took a road trip to Old San Juan for lunch at a local restaurant named, 'Manolin.' She loved it. "Emma." David went over to her. "Ready for some good coffee?" Her smile said a loud 'yes'.

"Let's go...you will love it there. It's called, 'Cuatro Sombras.'" "Oh, good...yes! I need a good cup of espresso. After that though, I want to take pictures in 'El Paseo de Sombrillas,' with the colorful umbrellas I see everywhere." They took tons of beautiful pictures, they drove past the ocean, stopped at 'El Morro,' took pictures there too, and headed home. She had a great day with her family on her favorite island.

Her plan was to stay with her sister, Raquel, and then a few days with David so she could spend time with her nieces and nephews as well. That night she settled in with her sister while her niece, Val made them hot cocoa.

"Raquel, look." She showed her an email from Mitch on her laptop. "Oh no, Emma. He's targeting Lyla again." In the email he was venting to Emma about Lyla. His words had no context. He was just trying to get her attention, so she wrote him to not contact her.

She called Lyla to get a feel of what was going on. "Hi, Honey. How's college?" Emma heard in Lyla's voice that she was crying. "Lyla, Honey? What happened?" Lyla took a breath, and in between the tears she managed to answer her mother. "Dad, keeps bothering me, Mom. He keeps calling me and screaming at me for no reason." Emma's heart couldn't take it anymore. "Lyla, you have the right to not answer him. Do you want me to talk to him?"

"No, Mom! It's worse when you talk to him about me." She might have freed herself from Mitch, but Lyla, as a daughter, felt attached.

A week later she returned to New York, refreshed and ready to restart her life. She returned a call she missed from Mitch to see if she could calm him down, and get him to stop bothering Lyla.

"Hi Emma...you okay?" "Never better," she wanted to say, but instead replied, "What's up, Mitch? Why did you email me?"

"Emma, I can't just not talk to you. I love you...come home." She never understood how he could be so mean to Lyla, and then ask her to come home as if her daughter's pain wouldn't affect her.

"Mitch, what happened with Lyla? Remember you emailed me about her?"

"Nothing, why? Did she say something?" "Lord give me patience with this man," Emma cried out. No, Mitch...you brought it up to me in your email. So, what happened?"

"Nothing, she didn't answer my calls and I'm paying for her phone. She should answer." "Why are you calling her so much? She's in college - studying. Maybe she was in class, Mitch. Also, why would you email me about that? Why are you calling her anyway?" she demanded. She's 21 years old for gosh sake...a woman! There is no need for you to be calling her...besides you still make her nervous." "Oops!" she thought. Ugh, why did I let that slip? She knew Mitch would be defensive about that and call Lyla.

"What the F do you mean, I make her nervous? What the F are you talking about? Wait until I get a hold of her! I give her everything! I'm going to disappear, and neither one of you will ever find me!" Emma hung up on Mitch. He called back, but she didn't answer. She quickly called Lyla and told her not to answer her phone. She needed to help Lyla get stronger so she would understand that it was okay not to respond to Mitch. He was a narcissist! She could ignore him or anyone else that bothered her. It was time to pray as it appeared that the craziness was not over. This was one journey she could not manage alone. She prayed for Lyla that God would protect her and give her strength. She prayed for her daughter to not lose her loving self. She was becoming angry.

AFTERMATH

A few months into the break up, Emma felt a sense of freedom she never knew before. She also felt like she still had a lot of pressure and baggage. There was a heaviness inside her that she didn't understand. It was time for reinforcements...she needed a friend.

"I'm sorry I pushed you away...I didn't mean to. I'm trying to make up with my family too. I don't know what happened to me, but family is everything to me now." Tracey understood.

"I forgive you...I was just waiting for you to call. Finally!" she laughed, which eased Emma's pain.

"Let's order in." Emma was happy to have her friend back. She didn't know what freedom meant, but she knew one thing...having a good friend, and being close to family was part of it.

They talked while enjoying their lunch. "Tracey, why do I feel so anxious and depressed all the time? Shouldn't I be good now? I'm not with him anymore. Little by little he stopped bothering me." Tracey looked at her like she had two heads.

"Okay Emma, look at me. You have just been through years of emotional abuse, narcissistic abuse - I read all about it and it is shocking. You can't expect to be okay so soon. Abuse is abuse and you both have internal bruises. God will help you through this, but Honey, take one step at a time. That was a tough life, not to mention everything else piled onto it." Emma looked at Tracey in a whole new light, and smiled at her.

"What?!" Tracey asked Emma. "Well, well, well...where have you been hiding all that wisdom?" Tracey laughed.

"Oh, you know, here and there." They both laughed. "Listen, I knew what you were going through, so I did a lot of research on it, and I waited for you to be ready. I knew you would eventually be ready. I know you, Emma, it almost took too long. I was about to intervene. You know I'm right, Emma." Yes, Emma knew.

"I do know what you mean. I was thinking of seeking professional help. I need some guidance. I'm also going to look for a new church. Boy, do I need that! I was also thinking of signing up for a gym and guitar lessons. I want to start writing again too...oh, and I want a Pomeranian puppy...maybe two." Tracey laughed and faced her.

"Okay, girl look...one thing at a time. Jeez, you have like years of pent up energy. You will get to do all those things, just be patient."

"Okay fine...one Pomeranian at a time." Tracey hugged her longtime friend.

Emma signed up for guitar lessons like she said she would, hired a trainer, ordered healthy food boxes, and bought a Pomeranian puppy. She was starting to feel happy again. She wanted to share her joy with her dad... something she couldn't do before.

"Hi Dad, guess what? I signed up for guitar lessons! I can't believe I never paid attention to when you played." "Oh, that's awesome, Honey. Good for you! I'm so proud. Just be patient...you will learn." Emma knew it would be difficult, since she currently lacked focus and patience. Since leaving such a controlled life with Mitch, she felt like she was learning, living, and seeing the world for the first time. She wanted to do everything. "I can't wait to see you again, Dad. I'll be there soon."

A few days later her sister, Katie called her. "Hey, what are you doing? How is it going since the break up?" Emma had distanced herself from everyone so it was time to reconnect. She was happy to hear from Katie.

"Hey, I'm good. I'm at the mall shopping for a coat. Mitch still has my stuff." Emma hadn't thought about that part yet. She had left nearly everything at home with Mitch. "What?! Well, go get it! That's your stuff,

Emma!" Katie sounded angry. "Oh, I just haven't gotten to that yet." She didn't want to tell her that she was afraid to reach out to Mitch. In the beginning, he was nice and accepting, but then he became angry with her and stopped calling.

"Well, you shouldn't spend money on new stuff when you already have everything." Emma knew she was right. It was time to face Mitch. "You're right! I'll have to set up a day to go and get everything." Katie offered to go with her. She wasn't going to lose her sister again for the third time, and wanted to be there for her now. "Well, let me know what he says, okay? I'll talk to you soon." Emma agreed and decided to reach out to Mitch that afternoon by emailing him. She couldn't bear to hear the sound of his voice.

"Mitch, let me know when it's a good day to pick up my things." That's all she wrote. Mitch wrote back almost immediately. "What things?! Everything is gone!" "Ugh," Emma thought. Why did I think this would be easy? She responded, "What do you mean it's all gone? I need my things, my coat, my boots - winter is coming." He responded again. "There is nothing here of yours, and do not come by...I have changed the locks." Wow, he was taking this to a whole other level. What a terrible thing to do by a grown man. She took a moment to pray since she had learned what she should do now when she was feeling down. God would know what to do, and would tell her. In the meantime, she had no choice but to spend money she didn't have to buy new clothes, a coat, snow boots, and everything else including some kitchen things she had dropped off at his house. She canceled the trainer and guitar lessons until she could figure out her next move.

"Tracey, how can he be so selfish? It's not like I was asking for my jewelry and things that are in the safe. I literally was just asking for a coat." Tracey was angry. "Listen to me Emma, don't apologize for his behavior. Everything is yours whether or not he bought it...they were gifts. The engagement ring too which you have been wearing for like 12 years is not to be given back. He didn't propose so that was a gift too. I have a feeling you will not be getting that back either. Look, if he is what you said he is, a narcissist, then you can forget it. You might have to go to the house with an officer." Emma did not like the sound of that. She wanted him to give her what was hers without a hassle.

"Why does he have to be so difficult?" Tracey looked at her. "Because you left him, Sweetie." Emma knew that was true. "I know, but I left to save myself. Clearly that is not how he is taking it." "Also, Emma, I know you are not married legally, but you guys shared a life for 20 years. Didn't you buy things for the house? Everything belongs to you too!" Emma thought about how much she had put into the relationship with Mitch, including the abuse, the cheating, the lying and everything else he put her through, and he couldn't even return the minimum of things.

"You're right, Tracey, but I checked. 'Common Law Marriage' doesn't exist in NY or NJ. I am literally leaving this relationship without even so much as a form from my own kitchen." She didn't feel angry... she felt sad and disappointed. She had given him so much, basically living for him. She decided to write to him again to give him one more chance to do the right thing.

"Mitch, I am not going to pretend I know how you feel, but we were together for a very long time. The least you can do is return my things. If you don't want me to pick them up, then ship them to my apartment." His response was just as negative as the first one.

"Mitch, you have to understand that I left to save me. You were mistreating me, you were abusive, you lied and cheated. If I did that to you, you would have the right, no question." He only responded that he wouldn't send her anything, and added that he hopes she has fun with her new life and paying for their daughter's college tuition. She nearly fainted. Now she was stuck with paying her tuition? She didn't have the money for that!

"God, please! Do you see this? I know and You know this is wrong of him. Please touch his heart and make him do the right thing, Lord. Also, help me not to hate, but to forgive. I can't live with this anymore...I need to let it go."

Emma dropped it and instead made herself busy by signing up for college. If she was going to be stuck with Lyla's college loans, she would have one of her own as well. College was another thing that she put off because of Mitch. She was excited to start fresh...college and a new apartment. She decided to give God the bigger problems. She definitely could not handle Mitch, so she chose to be happy instead...even if that meant starting from scratch. What was freedom if she held onto her past?

"Hey Mom, how are you doing?" Lyla called her mother daily to check on her. "I'm good love...finally free." Lyla sensed something in her mother's voice. "Mom? What's wrong?" It was time to tell Lyla the truth about college.

"Lyla, honey...have you spoken to your dad?" "Yeah, he said he was dating someone called Irene. I didn't want to tell you, but I figured you should know." Emma couldn't believe her ears. He was still seeing that woman, so why was he giving Emma such a difficult time? "It's okay, Lyla. Irene is the girl from before."

"Oh Mom, I'm sorry...I didn't know. I was just glad that he might leave you alone. That's so wrong." Emma felt anger again, but not as much anger as she knew her daughter would feel after she told her about school, but she had to.

"Lyla, there is something else...Dad is making me pay for college." Lyla went silent. "But listen Honey, I will be okay. You are nearly finished. I will pay what I can a little at a time."

"What?!" Lyla was furious just like Emma had predicted. "He told me I could go anywhere I wanted. I only chose the University of Texas in Austin, because he said he would pay for it. No Mom, this can't be happening! Not only that...he made me take a double major! No...no way! Why is he such an asshole, Mom?!" Emma took a deep breath. "No, Honey...language. It's okay, we can do this. Don't double major if you were only doing it to satisfy whatever he needed, but make sure you do finish."

IT'S NEVER TOO LATE

After a rough night for both girls, there was nothing they could do. The loan was in her name because he made her do it, but promised to pay her directly. Her things that she could possibly sell were in the safe in his house. She no longer had the house or anything in it, and her finances were going down the tubes.

Lyla decided to never speak with him again. He didn't act like he loved her anyway, so why should she? Emma couldn't blame her after what he put her through. She couldn't believe that she chose to raise her little girl with him. "Mom, don't feel bad. We went over this - you didn't know. He was nice for a few years, or at least pretended to be." Emma knew it wouldn't be very easy to get rid of that kind of guilt, but nothing was impossible with God.

It was a year into the breakup when Mitch decided to send Emma her things, probably because Irene was tired of seeing Emma's things lying around. She didn't care...at least she got back most of it and her jewelry too. "Thank you, God for making that happen." She felt like that chapter closed, but she had some feelings to deal with so she called her therapist to see her the next day after work. Emma started to see a therapist a few months into the breakup...it was much needed.

"Tara, I just don't know how to feel. I mean,I'm free…so why do I feel like crap?" Tara was a kind, young therapist, who Emma confided in pretty quickly. She knew that the only way to get well was to be truthful, so she was.

"Emma, just remember the first time you came to see me. You could barely get a word out...you were crying so hard. You have come a long way, so please don't feel like you haven't made any progress." Emma remembered that first day. Tara had asked her why she was there and Emma cried hysterically - she couldn't even speak. The reason was clear, therapist or not - no one had ever asked her how she was feeling, and if they did, they just wanted to hear, "I'm well, thank you." "Also, Emma, you have been through many, many years of trauma - not to mention Kyle and your grandfather - it's a lot, Emma. You have not had a chance to breathe. Then Mitch goes and lives with the mistress, doesn't return your things, and your daughter is a woman now. You didn't have a chance to make it up to her as a child, and now you're alone. Give yourself a break."

"I just feel like I am not doing enough, but yet I am doing so much now that I am free." Tara smiled. "You should be proud of yourself. You have direction and a desire to live. You have come a long way. Also, you told me that he took over your life, so of course, you are going to feel like you are not doing enough. He took over every breath, every minute of your life." Emma agreed.

"True, he filled every minute of my life with something. It's like he had another mind...another body to use besides his. That really is crazy, Tara. No wonder I feel exhausted."

That's sure is narcissism at its best, Emma."

"I need to focus, and continue praying so God can show me my path and my purpose." Tara smiled. "One thing I know for sure," Emma said. "What's that, Emma?"

"I don't think I will ever date again." They both laughed. "You will meet someone someday, when you are ready. It's never too late." Maybe not, Emma thought, but she had too many things in her life to do. Meeting someone was not on the top of her list...at least not until she was complete by discovering who she was and what she wanted.

Emma left her therapist's office feeling hopeful. She was realizing more and more how her life made sense now, and all of the good she wanted to do with it. Healing would take some work, but she had God in her life now. She found a local church, participated in events, and made new girlfriends...something she was never able to have before. That night, she gave God special thanks.

"Thank You, God for waiting for me. Starting my life over at 47 years old is not ideal, but there is nothing I can do about that. I should have listened sooner and made better choices. Thank You, for showing me why I made certain choices, so I don't make them again. Thank You, for helping me trust again. I have some amazing friends now. God, I don't know why this happened to me...why my life was so chaotic, and now I can only hope that I learn from each moment and move forward. I'm sure my purpose will be known to me soon. Forgive my anger over how I lived with Mitch and how he is treating me now. I will never know why someone like that could get away with what he has. Lord, there is something I have to do...I just don't know what. I trust that You will tell me and guide me to take action."

It didn't take long befor Emma headed back to Puerto Rico. She was catching up for lost time. Her brother, a Pastor, had written a book, and she wanted to attend a special service they had planned for him at his church. She was so proud of him. She was a writer too, had been writing her entire life - stories and poetry - but no one ever read them. She wrote to heal. Her brother wrote to teach. David had become a Psychologist and a Pastor, and now an author - a far cry from the little boy she helped raise. On this trip, Emma split her time between her siblings, and even stayed with her father for a couple of days. She was in heaven! Seeing her dad change his life the way he did, being a worship leader at church, and dedicating his time to his family gave her hope. She loved seeing him like this.

"Yes, David please! I want to go on a road trip and look for 'alcapurrias' to eat." Her brother knew she loved the island and everything on it. He promised them a road trip, and Emma was thrilled about it. They played old music on the radio, laughed about old times, and she played in the backseat with the kids.

"Emma..." Her sister-in-law looked at her in the back seat. "Yeah, Liz?" Liz was quiet for a moment. It was like she wanted to tell her something, but was changing her mind. "Liz,what?" David looked at his wife...he knew her well. God had a message for Emma through her. "Liz, tell her - don't hold it in." She sighed and Emma was curious. "I didn't want to say anything, but..." Ugh! The suspense, Emma thought. "Well... I feel like you are going to write books for women..." Now it was Emma who was being quiet. She saw her brother glance at her through the rearview mirror and smile.

"Umm, what?" She turned to Emma again. "Yes, you have to write to help women." "Help them with what?" she wondered and said, "I don't understand." Liz continued. "Do you write?" "Yes, I write." Liz didn't know that. "Well, you need to write to help women...I felt that in my heart." "Wow," Emma thought. Maybe this was her purpose. To write about what she'd gone through and how God helped her to be free to heal. Only a person who had suffered through certain situations should or could talk about them. She felt light...she now knew.

"Wow, God. Is that why you sent me to college...to be better prepared? I s that why I suffered through certain things in life, so I could talk about them later?" Everything was starting to make sense.

The next day was the ceremony for David's book at church. They were dressed up nicely. Her dad and sister Raquel were there and they were happy for this moment. David and his family were sitting up on stage while the pastor spoke proudly about him and his family, and they prayed over the book. While David's family were being prayed over, the person praying suddenly turned to Emma and called her by name. Emma opened her eyes and looked up at that person in shock. That's when she heard it again; "Emma, you have to write books to help women." She couldn't believe it. "Okay, God. Give it to me straight," she thought. She was ready to begin her journey. God spoke to her through this person with such love that Emma finally felt important and valued; valued enough to work for God. He told her that afternoon that He knew her heart. He read her stories and poems, and she needed to share them.

"Dad, did you hear that?" Al hugged his daughter. "Yes, I'm so proud of you. You have a gift Emma, use it. This is the time. All that pain, all those experiences, and how God freed you from it...just like He freed me." She was excited about her life. She still had emotional things to deal with, but this time she would let God help her. "God, if you want me to do this, I need healing quickly because I am a mess. I don't think I qualify to help anyone in this condition...Jesus please."

She spent the afternoon with her family celebrating her brother's success. They talked, ate and sang like usual. She was happy to be able to do this on a regular basis now that she was free.

"The difference now, Raquel, is that I am going home free. Home to my home, my things, my job, my school, and to new adventures." Raquel was happy for her sister. "Now all you have to do is move here...start your journey here!" She laughed at that.

"Yeah, I wish. I would if I didn't need this job, because I have to pay for the loan Mitch left me with. It's like I still feel trapped, or he tried to trap me with it, but I will not let it get to me. I gave that worry to God! I can't deal otherwise." Giving her worries to God was new for Emma and it gave her peace knowing that God was real and that He really would take care of her. She had been through too much already. She didn't need this burden too.

"I think in essence that New York is where He might want me since this loan is pretty much keeping me there, but I don't know yet, Raquel."

"Yes, I get what you mean. You don't want to live in New York, but you kind of have to stay there for now. We will see what your future brings... including a new love!" Emma gave her a look.

"Uhhhh, no...not yet!" They both laughed. It was so great to be here away from all the chaos, but it was time to say goodbye once again.

Emma had a new life to begin, a new journey to enjoy, and apparently a book to write. There was some unfinished business with Mitch, but she would have to pray and explore her options to figure out her next move. For now, she would enjoy the moment and give God the control which meant that everything would be okay.

Printed in the United States
By Bookmasters